Across the roof, Batman shook his head slowly.

He'd recognized Catwoman as soon as she moved toward the pipe. He watched her stand in his full sight and fuss with the rope. He had a pretty good idea what she meant to do.

Too bad. He'd have to stop her. He figured he could wait until she started to move—no sense risking the noise of a scuffle.

Without acknowledgment, they both crept forward. They saw what they wanted to see: a solitary walker headed this way in the next crosstown block and a high-riding 4-by-4 rolling blind and mute around the corner.

Catwoman gathered her rope. Batman pressed his hand against the cement capstone on the wall, muffling the sound of the thermite with his gauntlet. This wasn't in anybody's script. Catwoman drew her legs up onto the capstones and dared a glance over her shoulder. Their eyes met for an instant and they could no longer pretend to be unaware of each other.

Then all hell broke loose as the windows of the 4-by-4 came down and muzzles pointed outward . . .

Catwoman

ATTENTION: SCHOOLS AND CORPORATIONS

WARNER books are available at quantity discounts with bulk purchase for educational, business, or sales promotional use. For information, please write to: SPECIAL SALES DEPARTMENT, WARNER BOOKS,1271 AVENUE OF THE AMERICAS. NEW YORK, N.Y. 10020.

**ARE THERE WARNER BOOKS
YOU WANT BUT CANNOT FIND IN YOUR LOCAL STORES?**

You can get any WARNER BOOKS title in print. Simply send title and retail price, plus 50¢ per order and 50¢ per copy to cover mailing and handling costs for each book desired. New York State and California residents add applicable sales tax. Enclose check or money order only, no cash please, to: WARNER BOOKS, P.O. BOX 690, NEW YORK, N.Y. 10019.

Catwoman™
Tiger Hunt

Lynn Abbey and
Robert Asprin

WARNER BOOKS

A Time Warner Company

If you purchase this book without a cover you should be aware that this book may have been stolen property and reported as "unsold and destroyed" to the publisher. In such case neither the author nor the publisher has received any payment for this "stripped book."

WARNER BOOKS EDITION

Copyright © 1992 by DC Comics Inc.
All rights reserved. The stories, characters, and incidents featured in this publication are entirely fictional. All characters, their distinctive likenesses, and all related indicia are trademarks of DC Comics Inc.

Cover illustration by Dave Dorman

Published by arrangement with DC Comics Inc., 1325 Avenue of the Americas, New York, N.Y. 10019

Warner Books, Inc.
1271 Avenue of the Americas
New York, NY 10020

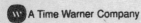 A Time Warner Company

Printed in the United States of America

First Printing: September, 1992

10 9 8 7 6 5 4 3 2 1

dedication:

To Brian Thomsen and Mel. White

Miles mean nothing
You were never far away when the crunch was on

Catwoman™

CHAPTER
One

*T*HE biggest problem with money was that somebody else always had it when you needed it.

Selina Kyle had little interest in money, except that she needed it to pay the rent, feed herself and her cats, and purchase those few essentials of modern life that could not be scrounged from the streets. Since arriving in Gotham City on her own at the age of sixteen, she had acquired money in a variety of ways, none of which was entirely legal or recognized as a career by the census bureau.

Selina took risks.

She'd woken up in a hospital more times than she cared to remember and, after one particularly brutal assault, she'd finally understood that in the East End, the grimy neighborhood she called home, only the predators survived.

So Selina Kyle became a predator—the Catwoman.

As Gotham City's colorful predators were measured, Catwoman was small time. On those rare occasions when the police or media took note of her exploits, they usually credited them to someone else. This lack of recognition neither displeased nor disappointed her. Felines were as aloof as they were fierce and independent, and cats—the plain ordinary alley cats from whom she took her name—survived by staying out of the way of the larger beasts whose environment they shared.

As Catwoman, Selina prowled her East End neighborhood, keeping it free of the lesser sorts of human vermin and earning the tolerance of her neighbors much as a prehistoric cat gained a warm, dry place by the fire in exchange for keeping the family cave free of mice and rats.

Selina and Catwoman shared a predictable life that left Selina as close to happy as she could imagine. Indeed, Selina's life fell short of purring bliss in just one small way—

Every so often, she needed money.

Every so often, Selina left her familiar territory—her neighbors never had the cash she needed, even if she had been willing to steal from them—and, dressed in inconspicuous mufti, stalked more affluent prey.

Every wilderness had water holes where a predator could lie in wait for its next meal. There were two types of water holes in the cityscape beyond the East End. The first type were freshly renovated buildings where slumlords-turned-renovators prepared traps for young, upwardly mobile professionals, naive newcomers who surrounded themselves with the best their money could buy, and knew precious little about security. On occasion Catwoman entered their porous domains to remove undefended jewelry and other small objects. Unfortunately, everything she took had to be fenced—a process that rarely produced more than ten cents cash for every dollar of swag, and exposed Selina to scrutiny from both sides of the law. All in all, she preferred to eliminate the middleman and steal cash.

Cash, in great abundance, was readily available at the second type of water hole: abandoned buildings where seminomadic drug gangs plied their trade. Selina roamed the sidewalks for several hours before she found the gutted, grafittied brownstone that would be this month's stalking ground.

A customized crimson 4 × 4—the current vehicle-of-choice among Gotham's appearance-conscious gang members—was parked in front of the target building. It had oversize wheels, a chrome-plated rollbar, and more top-mounted lights than a precinct cruiser. It also had a customized sound system and four sullen-faced attendants. It pumped the street full of what passed for music, which, by the time it reached Selina keeping vigil in a partially renovated building up the block, had been reduced to a thudding, monotone bass.

The owners of the 4×4 belonged to one of a handful of gangs doing the drug business in Gotham's marginal neighborhoods. A long step down from the million-dollar enterprises that kept Commissioner Gordon and the municipal police busy, the gangs waged ceaseless, brutal wars with each other. Abandoned buildings were the fortresses from which these hardened men oppressed a few unfortunate city blocks and sold their merchandise to a petty kingdom of hustlers and users. Once a day couriers brought the drugs in; once a day they took the money uptown.

Inconspicuously perched on a windowsill, Selina held her breath when another mobile sound system cruised up the street. She didn't know if the noisy black vehicle belonged to friends of the stationary crimson one or to mortal enemies. Elaborate greetings and gestures were exchanged; there was no gunfire. Selina let her breath out with a sigh. The black vehicle double-parked. Its speakers quieted. An exchange was made: a crate of money left the building, a crate of drugs went in.

Catwoman's teeth showed through Selina's smile as the black vehicle fired up its sound system and roared away. Her money worries were as good as over.

She went inside and, using a lumpy grocery bag for a pillow, curled up for a nap while the gang converted its fresh supply of drugs into cold, untraceable cash. The smile was replaced by a clenched-jaw snarl: the bass was just erratic enough to keep her awake. The fresh-painted walls surrounding her glowed yellow, amber, then red as the afternoon crept to an end. Streetlights flared; the sound never relented. Selina shed her street clothes and pulled the sleek, black catsuit over her body. Its hood and mask fit snugly around her head without dulling her senses.

She approached the building cautiously. The gang was undoubtedly armed with automatic weapons and keeping a lookout for the enemies it knew it had. The swaggering gangsters had little practice with the powerful weapons they brandished readily. They were almost as likely to shoot themselves or their friends as they were to shoot an enemy—especially a nearly invisible enemy whose specialty was hand-to-hand, close-quarters combat.

Ghosting down the trash-filled stairwell, Catwoman spotted the gang's upstairs lookout slouched against an empty window frame. A state-of-the-art assault rifle was propped against the peeling wall beside him. She knew the make of the rifle and that the paint was peeling, because they and the lookout were illuminated by a cool, flickering light. His attention was focused on the light on the windowsill in front of him; he had no idea there was someone perched on the bannister one flight up.

Catwoman gathered herself for the pounce. He'd never reach his fancy weapon; never know what hit him.

She froze instead.

A flicker of movement on another roof had drawn her attention. It was not repeated. There wasn't much for her memory to chew on, just the knowledge that something large and dark had been there and was now gone. That, however, was enough.

He was working the area and *he* was reason enough to scratch her plans, to head instead for shelter and stay there.

He was Batman.

Catwoman didn't fear the Dark Knight the way most criminals did. She wore a costume herself and was not impressed by his mask, his cape, or mystique. She'd eluded him before—even bested him—but he was a man obsessed with narrow definitions of right and wrong and it didn't pay to cross his bows—even when she needed money and had found the perfect people from whom to take it.

The lookout and the rest of his gang were safe—at least from her. But Batman's presence cast a strong, lingering spell across the jagged roofs. It prodded the lookout, who leaned forward, studying the roof where nothing untoward could be seen. His hand groped along the wall, seeking the rifle. He turned around. He looked up—

Damn!

He went for the handgun partially concealed in his pocket. The cards had been dealt; the hand had to be played.

Catwoman launched herself downward. Her hands locked around his neck. Her knees struck his chest. For a split second they were motionless, with him flat against the wall and her weight balanced against his collarbones. Then there was a snap, scarcely audible in the relentless music. Self-defense. Catwoman sprang away, landing on the balls of her feet. The lookout sank slowly to the floor, his head slumped to the side.

The motto on his T-shirt proclaimed "I'm too BA-AD to grow old."

Catwoman emptied his pockets and popped the heavy gold chain from his neck. He wasn't carrying enough to cover the rent, and once his unconscious body was discovered, this gang would blame another gang and the whole neighborhood would go into vengeance frenzy. He wouldn't remember after being knocked out. If Selina didn't get her money tonight, she could forget about getting it from anywhere around here for at least a week.

Damn.

She leaned out of the window. There were no brooding silhouettes hunched along the rooflines. Maybe *he* was gone. *He* wasn't necessarily hunting her prey. Heaven knew there was enough crime around here to satisfy them both. And she needed the money. Catwoman made a fist but stopped an inch short of smashing the flickering light with it.

A hand-held videotape player—trust the gangs to have the newest techno-toys. Trust their taste in videos to be slasher-porn.

Catwoman plucked the earphone cord from its socket and was astonished by the strength of the internal speaker: the woman's desperate screams made the unit vibrate in her hand.

There were knobs and buttons all over the unit. She pressed and twirled and was about ready to heave the thing into the night when the flickering blacked out and the screaming finally stopped.

Maybe she'd keep it. She stared at it, wondering if she'd ever use it, wondering what she could get for it. Catwoman couldn't waltz into a pawnshop with an ugly gold chain and a techno-toy, but Selina could. Added to the gold and the wad of cash she'd taken from the lookout's pockets, there might be enough—if Selina bargained hard. But if she bargained hard, the fence would remember her, and neither Catwoman nor Selina liked to be remembered.

Damn Batman for complicating her life!

A possible solution swept into her mind, washing away her anger: If Batman heard the screaming videotape, he'd drop everything and investigate. By the time Batman knew he'd been had, she'd have her money and be safe back home. It might work. She wrestled the unconscious lookout to the windowsill and let his body drop to the alley below. To her ears the crash was deafening, but if anyone else heard, they mistook it for a glitch in the sound system. Besides, the half-filled dumpster he landed in both softened his landing, and muffled the noise.

Returning to the apartment where she'd ditched her clothes, Catwoman deciphered the unit's myriad controls. Like any techno-toy worthy of its nameplate, it had more functions than it needed: a digital clock, a timer . . . A timer that could start the tape player at a preset moment. She fiddled with the controls, tested her theory, then grinned with smug satisfaction as she set her mousetrap—*bat* trap—on the fire escape.

The screaming would start in ten minutes—just when she'd be putting her foot through the drug gang's door. If he was anywhere in the neighborhood, he'd come a-running. He'd know he'd been snookered, but he'd never know why or by whom.

Catwoman's smile disappeared. Batman needed to know why and by whom. She wanted to paint a message on the wall with bloodred paint, but the workers had been careful and she had to settle for a thick carpenter's pencil. When the message was complete, she reset her trap beneath the handwriting and left to get her money.

The stairwell was empty. The gang didn't know they'd already suffered a casualty. Keeping to the shadows, Catwoman descended to the second floor, where voices could be heard through the din and the smells of kerosene and pizza were heavy in the air. A corridor door was open, throwing large shadows on the wall a few feet away. Catwoman studied the shadows, marking the number and locations of her prey: three that she could see, two that she could not.

Up the street, out of hearing, the techno-toy screamed.

Catwoman burst into the room at an angle, slamming into the guard by the door before he knew there was a problem. She stunned him with a punch to the solar plexus, then propelled toward the center of the room. The advantages of surprise and purpose belonged to her and she used them fully, taking out two more—the first with a chop across the windpipe and the second with a roundhouse kick to the chin— before the last two had a chance to bellow for reinforcements.

The street-side music finally stopped, replaced by shouts and staccato gunfire. There wasn't time to wonder who'd fired from where, or at what. Catwoman dove across the room at the larger of her remaining targets. He was reaching into his pocket, but he hadn't drawn a gun, nor had his companion. She seized her target by his shirt and spun him around, keeping his body between herself and the door while she rammed her knee into his crotch one, two, three times. His legs buckled, his eyes rolled back. He was deadweight, and crashed to the floor when she let go.

Less than a minute had passed since Catwoman burst into the room.

She leveled her gaze on the fifth punk—there were more thundering up the stairs; she'd worry about them when they came through the door—and observed, peripherally, that the kerosene lamp by which the gang had conducted its business had fallen over. Fuel glistened on the lopsided table and dripped over the edge. She didn't see flames, but flames were inevitable; the knife moving toward her was not.

First things first. Claws extended, Catwoman reached for the hand that held the knife. He got lucky—or maybe he knew something about fighting. Whichever, she clutched air.

"Get him!"

"El Gato Negro!"

"Black Cat! Black Cat!"

"Get him!"

The punks—her prey—saw the costume, but their prejudice kept them from seeing the shape inside it. They never understood that they were being slaughtered by a woman.

Surging inside the knife wielder's reach, Catwoman clouted him under the chin with a sweeping forearm then smashed her elbow into the side of his head as he went down. She looked straight into the eyes of the newcomer in the doorway. There were times for silence and there were times for bloodcurdling shouts. This was one of the latter. Her piercing war cry nailed the punk where he stood. The gun slipped through his fingers.

He didn't try to retrieve it. He and his companions beat a raucous retreat from the flames.

Catwoman watched for a heartbeat. The fire was spreading fast, but it was still less important than the money. She spotted a grease-stained, crumpled paper bag. When it was full, she headed up to the roof.

Selina was back home and out of the costume inside of twenty minutes. She began counting her money. There were three piles. The smallest would go into the poor box at the Mission of the Immaculate Heart: payment on a very private debt. The middle pile would keep her well fed and content for another month. The largest pile she shoved into a plain brown envelope.

Reaching under the sofa, she retrieved an old ballpoint pen. She printed in a neat, anonymous hand: Wilderness Warriors.

The Warriors were a small group of activists dedicated to

the notion that if the few remaining wild predators—the big cats, the timber wolves, the eagles, the grizzly bears, and the killer whales—were protected from the greatest predator of all—*Homo sapiens*—the wilderness and the world would be saved. They were one of many charities clanging the mission bell for Planet Earth, but Selina liked their name and the lion silhouette they used as an emblem, so she sent them her monthly surplus and told herself that the end justified the means.

CHAPTER
Two

*T*HE herd of emergency vehicles was thinning. The ambulances left first, followed quickly by the television crews. Who could blame them? The fire had looked promising for the late news, but there were no innocent victims—just body bags and stretchers filled with drug dealers and gang members. No relatives showed up to grieve photogenically. No neighborhood residents wandered by proclaiming that it was about time somebody put a torch to that place.

The fire trucks coiled their hoses and headed back to their stations. Most of the squad cars peeled off when their radios crackled to life with news of the next crisis. There were only two cars left. A black-and-white from the local precinct, and a Fire Inspector keeping watch a little while longer—just in case there was a pocket of fire left inside the smoldering wreck.

They thought they were alone on the scene. They weren't. Five stories up, on a roof, across the street, a black-shrouded, solitary figure watched, waited, and pondered what had gone wrong.

He'd passed through the neighborhood earlier in the night. He'd spotted the abandoned building for what it was: a drug depot, a gang's fortress. It was quiet enough, if you didn't count the four-wheeled boombox parked outside the front door. The gang wasn't going anywhere. He figured to bust it later on, after midnight. Before midnight he liked to stay loose and outside, ready to go where he was needed.

His parents died before midnight. All the years he'd been Batman, and all the years before he became Batman, Bruce Wayne never forgot how his parents were murdered on the Gotham sidewalks because no one was around to come to their defense. The Batman costume and persona were designed to put fear in the hearts of those who walked on the wrong side of righteousness, but Bruce had become Batman because the innocent had to be protected—especially when they got lost in the dark.

So when he'd heard the woman screaming in the next block, he'd gone immediately, tracking it down without the least suspicion until he beat down the door and saw the deceitful videotape player flickering in the middle of the empty room. Empty—except for the message scrawled on the virgin-white wall:

The body's not here. It's in an alley, up the street.
It's your fault—you on the rooftops—you made him jumpy
Drug gangs—terrorists and scum.
Killing them is no loss at all.
I take their money and put it to a better use.
But you don't understand that.
You won't mind your own business.
So you have to be tricked—for your own good.
While the Bat's at bay
The cat's at play.

Batman had crushed the tape player beneath his heel. He would have gotten rid of the message, too—if there'd been any white paint lying around. Catwoman was wrong. Justice must be served, and the end did not justify the means. Catwoman didn't understand—apparently could not understand—and that, in a tortured way, made her one of the

innocents. He suspected she was supporting herself by stealing from the drug gangs, where her crimes disappeared in the
statistical rounding. And his own passage through the area
had probably forced her hand. It didn't make what she did
right, but it did mean he didn't have to hurry.

Then Batman heard gunshots. Neither he nor Catwoman
carried guns. He had plenty of other gadgets hung on his belt,
but so far as he knew, Catwoman had only her claws and her
wits. She might be cornered. She might be outnumbered.
And she was innocent—at least more innocent than her prey.

Batman headed for the roof. He was standing there, pin-
pointing the source of the sounds and planning his rescue
assault, when he saw her sleek silhouette leap from an upper-
story window of the drug fortress. He'd cased out the area
earlier. He'd thought he'd known where she was headed, but
when he got there she wasn't. So Catwoman knew this part
of Gotham's jungle better than Batman did. That wasn't surprising: he knew she lived somewhere in the East End, and
that particular hellhole wasn't more than a quarter mile away
as the cat ran, or the bat flew.

He didn't pursue her. He'd spotted the flames by then,
and the rigid codes that, for him, separated right and wrong
mandated that he search for survivors. Justice wasn't served
at a barbecue. He was in the building, counting casualties,
when the fire trucks roared up. It was time to find the window
Catwoman used for her escape—the hardworking men and
women of Gotham's uniformed services had precious little
use for a loner like him. Life was less complicated when he
stayed out of their sight.

In some ways he and Catwoman weren't all that different.

Batman figured he'd stick around a while longer, until all
the uniforms were gone. He hadn't looked for the body in the
alley yet. It rankled him to think that she might have lied to
him. If she lied, she lost her protective innocence and he'd
have no choice except to hunt her down. So he waited on the
rooftop while the cops and the inspector joked with each other
over cold coffee and stale doughnuts.

"Jay-sus, will you look at that!" one of them exclaimed, gesturing with his pastry at the sky over Batman's head. "The Commissioner's got a burning gut again."

Batman craned his neck around, already knowing what he'd see: the beam of carbon arc lamp striking the clouds, framing the sign of the bat.

Catwoman could wait. The body in the alley would have to wait. Another servant of justice needed help.

There was no reason Batman couldn't walk through the front doors of City Hall and ride the elevator to Commissioner Gordon's office. The officers on duty here, while no less hardworking than their peers in the precincts, understood that the Commissioner's door was always open for the caped and masked man, and whatever their personal feelings about Batman, they viewed Gordon with a respect that bordered on awe. They knew the signal was beaming. They were watching for him, laying a few bets on who would spot him first.

Batman ignored the front doors, the back doors, and the basement loading docks. He used grapple lines to reach the broad ledge outside the Commissioner's office. After all, serving justice didn't rule out a few surprises. It wouldn't hurt either of them to laugh at a fundamentally harmless prank. Bruce Wayne could almost see his old friend spraying coffee across his desk when he heard his window opening rather than his door.

But Gordon's window opened silently, and he was too engrossed in his paperwork to notice which way Batman had come into the room.

"Ah—you're here. Good. Have a seat and let me fill you in."

A bit abashed, and grateful for the mask, Batman closed the window. Shrugging his shoulders reflexively to keep the cape from choking him while he sat, Batman settled into one of the leather armchairs. "Is this about the fire down below the East End—"

Gordon cut Batman off with a wave of his hand. "No, I

don't know about a fire, but it's not at all likely. Our problem isn't in Gotham City yet, but it's coming soon. Interpol and our own Federal security agencies had me in meetings all day; we just got them loaded on their planes and shipped out of here. Seems they've gotten wind of some newfangled terrorist group planning to come here to Gotham City to buy enough arms, ammunition, and ground-to-air Stinger missiles to outfit a small army.''

Batman leaned forward in his chair. His concern was clearly visible below the hard shadow of his mask. The Commissioner had his complete attention. "Who? There's no one in Gotham running that kind of arms race. Who's buying?"

"Didn't I ask them those very questions myself, and more than once, I assure you." Gordon tore a sheet of paper to shreds, crumpled it into a crude ball, and lobbed it at the basket. "But these are high-level bureaucrats, *diplomats*—not cops—and they're not going to tell me anything except that I'm supposed to turn over a hundred of my men to them—not to mention get them offices, computers, and their heart's delight of office supplies."

"Treating you like an errand boy. Coming in here like they're the grown-up and you're still the kid, eh? And talking about your men as if they were cannon fodder?"

Gordon exhaled his anger with a sigh. "That's the truth of it. Too sensitive for us *locals*. I thought at first they didn't have the facts to back their mouths up, but they showed me enough to make me think they're onto something. A couple wiretaps, a CIA briefing, an Interpol file filled with bad pictures and names I couldn't pronounce if I were drunk. Ever hear of Bessarabia or Bessarabians?"

Batman mouthed the word, making it sticky and tossing it into his memory to see what it caught. Nothing more than the vague sense that he had heard the word before. He shook his head in the negative, and Gordon was disappointed.

"Can't remember a thing myself either. Don't think they knew too much either. They all pronounced it exactly the same way—like a word they'd just learned yesterday. You know those types—they find their own way to pronounce

Monday, just so you'll know they've got an opinion they can't tell you about.''

Smiling wanly, Batman reached for the water pitcher on the corner of Gordon's desk and poured himself a glass. He hadn't expected to be inside tonight—especially not inside City Hall where the flow of political hot air kept the place overheated and stale. "I'll research it," he said after the water cooled his throat.

"I've got a staff of college-educated rookies camped out at the library. By tomorrow morning I'll know what Bessarabian grandmothers eat for breakfast. What I won't know is why they've come to Gotham City, where they're hiding, and what they mean to do before they leave.''

"You want me to find out?"

The answer was obvious, but the Commissioner hesitated before nodding his head. There wasn't a law-enforcement agency in the world that didn't owe a debt to one or another of the eccentric, sometimes inhuman, champions of justice. Gordon was privately grateful that Batman was simply eccentric—a human being beneath the polymer and dedication, who could still play a practical joke like coming through the window instead of the door. Even so, a few of Gordon's muscles always resisted admitting that a man in a costume could do things a man in a policeman's blue uniform could not.

"Track them down. Tell me where they are—then I'm going to put some of my best men on the job. I want this thing busted by Gotham's own." He stared intently at his fingertips. "You understand, don't you? Having you pull our bacon out of the fire time and time again . . . It's bad for morale. It's bad in the media—and this is going to get a lot of media. I can feel it in my gut.''

The phone rang conveniently, sparing Batman the need to reply, giving him another few moments to organize his thoughts and lay the groundwork of a comprehensive plan. If these Bessarabians were real, and he had no reason to believe they weren't, the combination of his computers and a little legwork would find them. He'd do that much for Gordon, and let the police force have the glory; he understood what Gordon said about morale. But the Bessarabians, as the buyers, were small potatoes on a larger plate.

He waited until Gordon hung up the phone and completed a notation in his daybook.

"Did your visitors drop any hints about the suppliers and sellers?"

Gordon closed the book slowly. Had he really thought he could invite his old friend here and not tell him the whole story?

"They mentioned a name: The Connection."

Batman slouched back in the chair, steepling his fingers against the exposed portions of his face, rendering his expression completely unreadable. The Connection . . . that was a name that made, well—connections. He was the ultimate middleman—whenever a buyer needed a seller, or vice versa, the Connection could make the market. The operation started up after the war—the big one, WWII—and for decades intelligence considered it a "what" rather than a "who": a loose association of wartime quartermasters, procurers, and scroungers doing what they did best.

There were files in the Batcave computer that continued to refer to the Connection as "it" or "they" in the stubborn belief that no one man could move so much matériel. Those documents also supposed that if the Connection were a man, he'd have come forward by now to claim his honors. Easily ninety-five percent of his activities were legitimate; some were downright heroic. The world had cheered when three bulging freighters steamed into Ethiopia with enough grain to feed the country's war-weary refugees for a month. The world, of course, had not known that buried deep in the wheat and corn was enough ammunition to feed the civil war for two years.

Bruce Wayne knew, just as he knew there could only be one mind behind it all. Maybe forty-five years ago it was a group; not anymore. No committee could generate the subtle elegance of the Connection's world-ringing transactions. But not even Bruce Wayne had a clue about the body or personality that went with the name. Other monikered individuals, including himself, had public faces and private faces, but the Connection—so far as anyone knew—had no face at all. A complete recluse, he'd never been fingered, not even when one of his operations went sour. If a description did emerge, it contradicted all previous ones—fueling the case of the committee-ists. Bruce Wayne was guiltily grateful that the Connection—though widely believed to be an American operation—scrupulously avoided washing its dirty laundry in the USA.

"They weren't positive," Gordon said when the silence became uncomfortably prolonged. "It's not the Connection's style to make a swap where our side has jurisdiction. They're leaping at the chance, I think, but they admit it might all be smoke and mirrors."

Massaging his cheeks, Batman shook his head. "The world's changing; it's already changed so much the sides are smudged. The Connection's got to change with it. I don't wonder that the Feds and Interpol are jumpy. There's a first time for everything—he's testing the waters."

Gordon took note of the singular pronoun. "You think it's one man, then?"

"I'm sure of it. One genius. He doesn't leave many traces, and when I find them, I'm always chin-deep in something else. But this time he's steaming right across my bows, and I'm going to find him." Batman's voice was calm and even, leaving no room for doubt.

The Commissioner drew a ring of arrows on his blotter, all pointing inward. "Remember," he said without looking up, "when the time comes, my men close the trap, not the Feds, not Interpol, and not you—"

Batman wasn't listening. A cool breeze was stirring the papers on Gordon's desk. Batman was gone.

CHAPTER
Three

*I*T was no accident that Batman's mind filled with maritime metaphors when he thought of the Connection. In this day of fiber optics and instantaneous communications, a good shipping line was still the best way to move contraband. Jet planes were faster, of course, and these days could carry just about anything if the need was great enough, and the buyer cared nothing about cost. Big planes, however, needed big runways and left big blips on radarscopes around the world. Refined drug operations, with their worth-more-than-gold cargoes, made good use of short-takeoff planes. But the Connection moved contraband by the ton, and for that an interchangeable string of rust-bucket freighters, casually registered in Liberia or Panama, and crewed by a motley assortment of nationless sailors, was a necessity.

Batman wasn't ready to leave the city for his cave and computers. Getting a lead on the Connection with pure legwork, prior to doing data research, was a long shot, but the night was young and his perambulations hadn't taken him along the waterfront in over a week. He made his way toward Gotham's deep-water harbor—one of the largest and safest in the New World and still a place where an isolated ship could come and go virtually unnoticed. He detoured briefly, cutting the corner of the East End and sating his curiosity behind the now-deserted and damp ruins of the abandoned building. A swift, but thorough, examination of the alleys revealed the bloodstained impression of a body dropped from above and the muddy stomping of the EMS crew that carted it to the street. Catwoman hadn't lied. He could put that out of his mind completely, and did.

The harbor's glory days were behind it now. Most cargo— legitimate or not—traveled in sealed containers that were hoisted from ship to truck or railroad flatcar at the massive new mechanized Gotham City Port Authority Terminal some twenty miles away. No one used the oceans for speed any-more. The great passenger ships and fast freighters had all been chopped up and turned into cheap, Asian cars. The lumbering oil tankers belched out their contents at oiling buoys anchored on the three-mile limit.

The big piers and wharves were crumbling mausoleums of days gone by. None of the ships riding beside them shoved identifying funnels above the rooflines. Batman climbed a rickety harbormaster's tower to get a better view, because things still moved here. These old docks were the biggest cracks in the system, and if the Connection were bringing something into Gotham City, the men working the night shift along the waterfront—the last of the stevedores—would have heard about it.

Expectations were rewarded. Midway along the dark line of piers, a dome of light marked the place where cargo was being manhandled with ropes, hooks, and shouts. Leaving the tower, Batman took an open path toward the activity, moving past the deep shadows, rather than through them, inviting a stranger to approach.

Contrary to common wisdom, there was no honor among thieves or any other criminal type. They were always eager to sell each other out, especially if they thought he—Batman— could be distracted with someone else's misdeeds. Word of his presence should have spread like wildfire, and since it was just about certain that somebody here on the waterfront was doing something he shouldn't be doing, it was equally certain that somebody would scuttle up with a tattletale rumor.

Mountainous bales of old clothes and musty newspapers stood in line, waiting for the crane to hook their rope-lashed pallets. Removing a small cylinder from his belt, Batman shone a finger of light across one of the bales. He recognized the logo of a respected international relief organization, and a series of destinations, in several languages and scripts, starting in the Bangladeshi port of Dacca and continuing on to Kabul in Afghanistan. Feeling suddenly lucky, he returned the cylinder to his belt.

There must be six million worthy souls in that misbegotten corner of the world willing to put to good use those things Americans had used once and thrown away. There were also a half dozen different insurrections operating there, and Batman could practically smell the armaments packed—unbeknownst to the relief organization—in the middle of each bale. Although the Connection didn't transship through American ports, he'd certainly want to know if someone else was. When Batman spotted the silhouette of a solitary man leaving the pier area at a brisk pace, he gave chase.

Batman caught up with the walker in the concrete fields beneath the waterfront highway. Not wanting to stage the confrontation in the open, he circled wide and waited until his quarry was striding down a deserted warehouse block. Batman didn't say anything. The mask, the cape, and his thou-shalt-not-pass stance spoke louder than any words.

He got a good look at the man he'd been following. Dark-haired and powerfully built. About thirty, give or take a handful of years. The stevedore's age was hard to guess; his face was puckered with a series of long, thin scars. Because of where he'd been earlier in the evening, Batman's first thought was that the man had been mauled by a big cat, but he rejected that thought. The scars weren't quite parallel, and there were at least six of them. Somebody'd worked this fellow over with a steel whip.

"I got nothing to do with you," the scarred man said with a sneer. "You ain't king of the jungle around here."

Batman wasn't entirely surprised that his quarry was unimpressed by appearances. It took a certain kind of man to live with scars like that; it took a certain kind of man to survive the getting of them. "You were working on the pier. Loading that freighter for Bangladesh?"

"No, I was checking my yacht for a friggin' regatta." He took a step sideways; Batman moved with him. "We don't keep regular hours," he explained, as if talking to an exceptionally dense child. "The boats come and go with the tides. That one's going to leave about four A.M.—if that's all right with you, I suppose."

"I'm looking for someone who ships a lot of freight to places like Bangladesh—places where the people are poor and needy and the customs inspectors are conveniently blind—"

"Don't know what you're talking about." He veered the other way; again Batman stayed with him.

"Let's say I'm trying to make a certain . . . *connection*."

The light on the empty street came from a single halogen lamp at the far end of the block. But Batman was angling for a reaction, so he was watching when the dark eyes lost focus and pulled sharply to one side. He didn't need a polygraph to know when a man was getting ready to lie. He began feeling very, very lucky.

"What kinda connection? There's things come into port sometimes. Maybe I hear about them. Maybe I don't. It depends." The scarred stevedore shrugged his shoulders and slipped a hand under the waist ribbing of his wool sweater.

Batman knew what was coming, and how he'd react: carefully. Whoever this guy was, he looked to be useful. "What's your name?" he asked on the off chance that an answer would be forthcoming along with the knife.

"Call me Tiger."

It wasn't a knife, but one of the hooks stevedores used to maneuver cargo pallets while they were swinging through the air. An ordinary hook could puncture a man's lungs. This one had been filed and sharpened, and Tiger whipped it through the air like a pro.

Dodging the first two sweeps, Batman took the measure of the man and his weapon before closing in. His costume protected him from things inherently more dangerous than eight curved inches of sharpened steel, but his partially exposed face was open to mistakes and punishment. It didn't pay to be careless. Nor would it pay to disable his attacker. Batman employed an oriental martial arts hand-to-hand technique, keeping his forearms constantly in contact with Tiger's, making his slash wide and pushing him steadily backwards until his back was against a proverbial wall.

As soon as Tiger felt brick behind him, his eyes glazed. He put all his strength and effort into a mighty sweep at Batman's jaw. The masked man expected just such an over-commitment of energy. He got his weight underneath Tiger's, shoving upward slightly, outward mostly, and getting his gauntleted hand over the haft of the weapon just before Tiger went flying along the pavement.

He landed on his butt, with both palms flat on the ground beside him and a dumbfounded expression twisting his face. He saw his weapon in Batman's hands, and confusion transformed to white-hot rage. Batman took a stride forward, closing the fight distance before Tiger could launch an attack.

"Don't be a fool, Tiger," Batman said, darkening the man with his shadow.

Tiger scrabbled backward before getting to his feet. "You got nothing, Bat." He glanced over his shoulder getting ready to run—but not, Batman noted, toward the pier.

"Tell me about the Bessarabians, Tiger." Batman played his ace in the hole, just to see what would happen.

"Don't know squat about the Bess-Arabs. Screw you and the sheepherders, too." He spun quickly on the balls of his feet and took off down the street.

Batman let him go. His mind was already chewing on new information. He hadn't expected a direct hit. Tiger had been smart enough to fudge his response to the Connection question, but he'd left himself wide open on the Bessarabians. The Bess-arabs. Maybe they were Arabs. Maybe they were sheepherders. The world was just beginning to wake up to the knowledge that the Islamic cultures were tribal, not national, and eager to fight among themselves in the absence of an infidel enemy.

He listened to Tiger's footfalls after the man rounded the corner, then heard the sound of a midsized diesel engine and jogged down the sidewalk himself in time to see the receding taillights of what appeared to be an express parcel delivery van—complete with a satellite dish and antenna mounted on the roof.

Tiger caught his breath on the metal steps leading up to the driver's pedestal-seat. The encounter had been his first with a bona fide Hero. He felt he'd handled the occasion well, all things considered. A boy couldn't grow up in Gotham City without seeing Batman and his cronies—even if that boy grew up as Tiger did, on the East End streets where a television was something you watched in front of a pawnshop window. Of course, a boy like Tiger grew up knowing that for every Batman, there were a dozen villains. He knew all their names, where they were, what had happened, which few had never been brought down.

He studied their failures, because he was never going to make their mistakes. The time was coming when there'd be a new name front and center in all the media. The Tiger. Him. It was his life's ambition—the only thing that had sustained him during the lean years before he met the man in back. When he had tried too hard, rather than smart, and ran afoul of a no-name bookie with a coil of razor-wire and a grudge. Those days were behind him. If Tiger had had any doubts, he purged them while he chiseled his encounter with Batman into his memory, enhancing the good parts, smoothing over the bad moments until they were gone.

He was Tiger. He'd been rousted by Batman—who only rousted important guys. He hadn't cracked, not the way some punks did, spilling their guts the moment they saw that mask and cape. He'd told the Bat off, fought him to a draw, and left in the time and manner of his own choosing. He'd lost his weapon. That was hard to enhance or smooth over, until he decided that a hook wasn't a weapon, it was a tool, and tools were destined to be discarded once their usefulness was gone.

The man in back had taught him that.

The driver wheeled the van onto one of the uptown avenues. He used its tanklike bulk to commandeer the middle lane and picked up speed to get in synch with the traffic lights. They were bouncing through the potholes at about twenty-five miles an hour when the van erupted with an earsplitting whine. Gripping the wheel one-handed, the driver wrestled bright yellow foam earmuffs over his head. Tiger ground his teeth together, winced, and held on for dear life as the van bucked and shook.

It took thirty seconds to acquire the signal, thirty seconds that lasted a lifetime. Then it was over, reduced to a barely perceptible vibration beneath Tiger's sweat-slicked palms. The driver left his earmuffs on. Tiger grabbed ahold of the sliding door and stepped into the bright fluorescent light filling the back of the van.

"You were late. You almost missed us."

The light wasn't natural. It radiated from the walls, the ceiling, and the floor. Coming in from the night, it made Tiger's eyes water. He squinted and sniffed, and waited for his vision to clear.

"But I didn't," he asserted.

The Connection remained blurry behind his massive black desk. A soft-featured man on the far side of fifty, with pale hair the same color as his pale skin. Tiger's heart skipped a beat—he thought he recognized the face. He did—a congressman from Nowhere, North Dakota, who'd just resigned his seat in disgrace. The Connection's idea of a joke.

The simple fact was, it didn't matter if Tiger's eyes ever got focused. Nothing here was real. It was all souped-up, high-tech gadgetry. The Connection never looked the same, sounded the same two times running, because the Connection wasn't here. God only knew where the Connection was when he beamed his holograph into the van. God only knew what he really looked like.

"Might I remind you that I despise arrogance even more than I despise carelessness?"

It didn't matter what the Connection looked like—or what he did to his voice. Tiger knew he was in the presence of his boss, and that was all that mattered. For now. Until he was The Tiger and ready to take over.

"We were shorthanded. I was working myself to get the stuff in the hold where it was supposed to be. Better to do it right and be a few seconds late." He jutted out his chin, faintly defying the holograph to disagree. He'd come up with an easy explanation if the metal detectors spotted that he didn't have his hook in his belt; *it'd gotten stuck in the last bale and he'd left it behind.* There was no need to tell the boss about Batman.

"You'll be shorthanded all the way through this next deal. I don't want any extra bodies nosing around, and no one on that ship who's not completely expendable."

"Gotcha."

"Is everything progressing according to the plan?"

It had to be a trick question. The Connection knew more about the plan than Tiger himself. But like all trick questions, it had to be answered correctly.

"Yeah, yeah. No problems. The Bess-Arabs are in town. I collected their collateral—two shit-painted pieces of wood in cheap gold frames. Who pays for this stuff, boss?" he asked rhetorically, not expecting an answer. "Anyway, I put 'em in the vault. I fly out the day after tomorrow; the ship picks me up tomorrow night. The merchandise is all sealed up already and waiting for us. I make sure it gets loaded on, then, ten days from now, I drop it over the side, put a radio buoy on it, and, bingo, I'm back in town to collect that third piece of shit. Eleven days and the deal's history."

The holograph nodded and shuffled papers, looking for one in particular, which it found. The effect was entirely convincing, except that there were no shuffling noises and the paper he held up was blank and faintly translucent.

"You're nervous, Tiger. Why?"

"I ain't, boss."

"We're bringing Seatainers of top-quality USArmy hardware—guns, ammo, and Stinger missiles—to Gotham City's front door and you're *not* nervous?"

"Yeah. No. It's like . . . Yeah, I'm nervous about it, but the plan's under control, so . . . No, I'm not. It's like that."

A considerable distance away, behind a real desk, in a real room filled with unique electronic and communications gear, a real hand fingered a real piece of paper. Three high-definition television screens provided an in-the-round view of Tiger swaying from side to side as the van bounced along its preset route. A cockpit full of telemetry displayed everything that couldn't be seen, from the absence of his favorite weapon in its sheath beneath his sweater, to the temperature gradient between his cold-sweating hands and his hot-sweating face. Even the way his gut was churning.

Tiger was nervous—exceptionally so—and lying about it. The Connection made a mark on the paper. Then again, Tiger was usually nervous. He wasn't as tough as he thought he was, or as smart. But he was tough enough, smart enough to have been a useful tool these last ten years. The Connection took a paternal interest in his employees; good men were hard to find in his line of work. They were all flawed in one way or another. He took it upon himself to see that the flaws didn't get out of control.

"How is Rose? Has she been behaving herself?"

The image on the television screens nodded. Telemetry showed that his pulse was skyrocketing and his gut was hard as lead.

"Yeah, yeah. She's okay. I'm the man. She's my woman. No problems."

Another mark on the paper.

"We were approached the other day by our contacts in Hong Kong. It's a small deal, but the exchange rate was interesting. It would appear that one of the Manchu emperors shared your passion for *Panthera tigris* and the Imperial collection has somehow survived. I've taken the liberty of selecting one of the choicer specimens."

The telemetry jittered before settling at much lower levels: visible proof that a man could be bought.

"It's in the desk. Take it with my thanks, my gratitude— for the good job I know you're going to do."

Tiger thrust his hands into the holographic desk. They struck something hard and fur-covered. He grasped it eagerly and withdrew a box cunningly constructed from a silver-gray tiger's skull. The excitement he felt holding it was spiritual and sexual, and transmitted to the Connection in his distant lair.

"I thought you would like it. How many do you have now?"

"A hundred and thirty-nine," Tiger said dreamily, stroking the stiff fur. "Any day now. Any day now the Tiger's gonna come."

The solid flesh of the real Connection shaped itself into a scowl that was not transmitted to the holograph. Tiger had been waiting ten years for his namesake. Someday he'd realize there was no Tiger spirit. Someday the Connection would have to kill him. But not quite yet.

CHAPTER Four

*T*HE day was perfect—bright and clear with a gentle breeze. The sky was azure blue and speckled with lines of wispy clouds. The morning radio personalities noted that Gotham City's one perfect spring day was occurring on a Wednesday, when the ordinary people who needed it most were least able to enjoy it. But to Sister Theresa Carmel, carefully twining a new ivy sprig around its older siblings, a beautiful day was a divine gift whenever it arrived.

Forty years ago, when the Order sent her to the mission they maintained here in the East End, Sister Theresa started scratching in the cement-hard dirt of the tenement courtyard. The heavy forged-bronze crosses that had been nailed to the front doors then were long gone—stolen some twenty years ago when a new breed of lost souls began moving in. Now everything had changed. The front doors themselves were made from steel, and there were bars over the dormitory windows. Those bars were the last things Sister Theresa saw each night before she fell asleep. She was as grateful for their protection as she was disheartened by the need for them.

But Sister Theresa's garden endured. The soil beneath

Gotham's debris wasn't dead; it had merely slept until a gentle, knowing hand awakened it. Now there were crocuses and daffodils by the dozens, with a dense mass of tulips rising behind them. The lilacs were budding with color. And the roses—Sister Theresa stepped carefully from one old cobblestone to the next, bent down and scattered the mulch with her large, knobby hands—had all survived the winter.

The rose she examined had been lifeless just yesterday, but was now showing crimson growth. It was a Peace rose, her favorite. She allowed herself the luxury of remembering the girl she had been when a young man gave her a single Peace rose with a diamond ring circling its stem. The years had eroded the pain; only the happiness was left, the warmth like the spring sunshine spilling down on the coarse black cloth of her veil.

She was surrounded by memories and light, but not lost within them. She heard the sparrows chirping and the distinctive click of metal against metal telling her that someone had entered the chapel where she, herself, was supposed to be. Something of the headstrong, romantic young woman remained with Sister Theresa as she dusted off her hands and left the garden for the chapel.

A young woman knelt before the altar. Her chin was pressed down to her breast. Her long blond hair fell in untidy loops and tangles across her slumped shoulders. Even at a distance, Sister Theresa could hear her anguished gasps of prayer. For a moment the older woman remembered herself. It was possible that this child had lost her beloved in a war— the constant war that was waged here in the East End.

With an unconscious smoothing of her veil, Sister Theresa Carmel pushed her memories out of her mind. She walked down the aisle armored with weary compassion and prepared for the worst.

"May I help you, child?"

The young woman sobbed with renewed despair, but did not move. Sister Theresa studied her profile. Her cheek was swollen with a fresh bruise. An older, darker one mottled her forehead, and there was a half-healed gash puffing out her lips. Not the worst battering the nun had witnessed, but that didn't help. She lowered herself into the pew and reached for the girl's hand.

"Tell me what happened. We're here for your welfare. For the welfare of your body as well as your soul."

The woman clutched her hands against her stomach. Fresh tears streaked her cheeks and were absorbed by her already damp sweater. She stared into a hidden place far below the floor and would not look up. She cringed when Sister Theresa touched her arm.

"Tell me, child," Sister Theresa said, hardening her voice. Most of those who came to the chapel were convinced that nuns were agents of divine authority who must be obeyed and who rendered judgment before they showed compassion. It was myth, of course, but useful at times. "You came here to tell me, and now you must do so."

"Sister Theresa . . . ?"

The young woman's head came up slowly. When their eyes met, and the nun recognized her, the battered woman lost the last shreds of her composure. Wailing, she flung herself facefirst into Sister Theresa's lap.

"Rose . . . Rose . . ." Sister Theresa stroked the dirty blond hair. "Rose, what happened? How did it happen?" Her own tears leaked onto her wrinkled cheeks. "Rose, why did you wait so long? You didn't have to suffer this. There's a place for you here, always. Always."

The girl didn't answer. She couldn't answer. The sound of Sister Theresa's voice—the almost forgotten but now remembered strength of it—allowed her to feel safe, but the illusion would be shattered if she moved. If she moved, she'd have to think. She would have to feel the terror and pain that had driven her back to this sanctuary. She'd have to answer Sister Theresa's questions.

Sister Theresa sensed the change as mindless despair gave way to denial. She knew the process too well not to recognize it. She stroked Rose's hair a few more times—for sentiment's sake—then took a deep breath and shoved the girl away.

"Tell me, Rose. Tell me the whole story. From the beginning. Don't leave anything out. Our Heavenly Father knows you can't tell these old ears anything they haven't heard before."

Rose drooped like an unstrung puppet. She squeezed her eyes shut, then opened them slowly. She'd run out of tears. A palpable aura of shame settled over her.

"Rose . . ."

Shiny sweat bloomed around the bruise on the girl's forehead. Her hands trembled no matter how tightly she clutched them together. Sister Theresa had seen it all before.

"What have you been using? How long since the last time?"

"It's not drugs," Rose whispered hoarsely. "I don't do drugs. Never. Ever." She tried to swallow, but choked instead and doubled over coughing.

Sister Theresa tightened her hands into fists until the closely trimmed fingernails dug into her palms. "Then what? Look at yourself! Your hair's dirty. Your clothes are dirty. You look as if you slept in the street. What have you been doing, if not drugs?" The nun waited a moment before answering her own questions. "Is it a man? Is it men? Is it, Rose?"

Rose swung her head silently, emphatically, from side to side.

The nun sat back in the pew. She cast her glance upward at the crucifix—a simple one of painted plaster now, but even that bolted to the wall so it could not be easily stolen—then brought it to bear on Rose's heaving shoulders.

Four years ago Rose D'Onofreo had come to the mission, a runaway from the routine horrors that passed for family life in the East End. Healing her body had been the easy part. Regular meals and undisturbed sleep worked the obvious miracles. But Sister Theresa's sorority thought they'd wrought a deeper miracle by healing Rose's soul as well. She went back to school, graduated, took secretarial courses. She got a nice job—a dress-up desk job—working for an East Ender who'd made good without forgetting where he'd come from. The sisters told themselves Rose was proof that their work was worthwhile.

To remind Rose that she was family, they pooled their meager allowances and gave her a golden rose on a delicate chain and gave it to her the day before she began her new life. Rose was all smiles and hope, but she never came back to visit. The sisters made excuses for her: Why should she come back? No *decent* young woman *should* walk these streets at any hour, day or night. They were experts at swallowing disappointment.

Sister Theresa couldn't keep herself from looking for the necklace, or realizing that it was gone. She couldn't keep herself from noticing that Rose's sweater was much too tight for anyone working in an office—though it was also much too expensive for anyone working the streets. The same was true of the skimpy skirt and lacy tights. In the dusty corners of her heart, Sister Theresa had disapproved of fashion since she, herself, had begun wearing a nun's habit—but she could tell street cheap from its fashionable uptown imitations. For the cost of Rose's clothes, the nuns could run the mission for a week. Sister Theresa Carmel shivered involuntarily.

"Where have you been? What have you been doing? Your job? Your apartment—?"

Rose remained curled over her knees, swaying back and forth. "I did . . . I tried . . ." she sputtered before succumbing to another spate of sobs.

The faint click of the opening door echoed in the chapel. Sister Theresa pressed her finger to her lips as another black-robed veteran of these little wars hurried down the aisle.

Rose? the newcomer mouthed, as surprise and dismay tightened her features.

Sister Theresa nodded, shrugged, and made room on the pew. Sister Agnes knelt instead, and wrapped her arms around the disconsolate young woman. Rose looked up into another dark, worried face.

Why had she come here? Whatever made her think that these woman—these wives of the church—could understand her world? She wished she hadn't come. She wished she was back in the bathroom, naked and staring at the battered stranger reflecting in the mirror. The bruises were the least of it. Couldn't they see that? Couldn't they see the shadow hanging over her, blacker than any bruise? She had thought that the shadow would be visible here. That the holy sisters would make the sign of the cross and drive it out. But they looked at her face, not the shadow. There was no help here. No hope.

Rose knotted her hand in her hair. She pulled until strands ripped loose and tears began to flow from her eyes again.

Sister Agnes recoiled in horror. "What's wrong with her?"

"She was at the altar when I came in. I asked her what was wrong. It's been all downhill since then."

"Is she hurt? Do you think we need an ambulance?" Sister Agnes asked.

"It's not the bruises hurting her. She's been beaten before—God help us all—and didn't come to us. No . . . something's struck her soul. It's still there."

Rose heard the words she longed to hear, the words confirming her darkest fear and shame. The voice of her God-given conscience wanted to confess everything, but when she opened her mouth a single, scarcely human scream came out instead.

The two nuns swiftly crossed themselves, glanced at the crucifix, then at each other.

Sister Theresa got unsteadily to her feet. "In the garden." She got a hand under Rose's shoulder and motioned for Sister Agnes to do likewise. The mission walls were echoing with the footfalls of the other nuns responding to the crisis.

Fresh air and sunlight helped a bit, but it was the sight of unfamiliar faces that restored Rose's sense of self. She tamed her hair and restored order to her clothing with expert gestures. She faced all of them, and none of them.

"I—I—I don't know what came over me." Her voice, ragged at the start, was impenetrable by the end.

Knowing looks flashed among the nuns. This, too, was familiar and expected. East Enders could hide the most profound despair in a heartbeat; it was their survival camouflage. They had skills a professional actor would envy. Rose's performance might have worked on the streets, or on stage, but it failed to impress her audience in the garden. And she knew it.

"I haven't felt too good for the last few days," she said lamely, brushing her forehead as if checking for a fever. "I guess I got the flu. The flu can make you crazy. I saw it just last week on television—"

"Rose."

The new voice made all of them—Rose and the avowed sisters alike—swiftly examine themselves within and without. Mother Joseph rarely came downstairs. She lived on the phone, dealing with the morass of Gotham's so-called Social Services Department and wrangling the donations that kept the mission alive. She seldom left her office while the sun was shining, and it was never good news when she did.

"What's going on here? One minute there's a banshee in the chapel, the next you're all dawdling in the garden."

"Rose came back," Sister Theresa admitted in a small voice.

Mother Joseph folded her arms in front of her. She had the patience of a saint, or a stone, and by the angle of her head let Rose know she was prepared to wait for the Last Judgment, if necessary, for an explanation.

A wave of guilt and shame broke over Rose. She felt naked and worthless—but she was used to that. If Rose had allowed feeling worthless to stop her, she'd never have made it to kindergarten. "I made a mistake," she said flatly. "I shouldn't have come here."

You couldn't lie when you were naked, but there were a thousand kinds of truth. Squaring her shoulders, Rose started for the street. She hadn't gone two steps when Beelzebub, the mission's battle-scarred tomcat, streaked past. Anyone might have been startled by the sudden movement. Almost anyone might have yelped with surprise. But Rose was wide-eyed, stark-white terrified.

Beelzebub yawned and stretched himself across a sun-warmed stone, looking for all the world like nothing had happened. Sister Theresa became aware of someone staring at the back of her neck. She turned to face Mother Joseph.

After so many years together, the veterans didn't need words. The set of Mother Joseph's features, the subtle movement of her right eyebrow, all conveyed a very clear set of orders.

Sister Theresa slipped her arm gently, firmly around Rose's waist. The young woman blinked, but her eyes were as wide and frozen as they'd been before.

"You haven't forgotten our old midnight caller, have you?"

Rose closed her eyes. The acute phase of the panic attack ended; she began to shiver. "I want to go home now," she whispered.

Sister Theresa felt Rose's heart pounding through their combined clothing. "You should sit in the sun a moment and get your breath." She tried, and failed, to turn the girl around.

"No. I want— I'll feel better when I'm back where I belong."

Scowling slightly and getting a solid grip on the waistband of Rose's skirt, Sister Theresa held her back. "We'll call you a cab. You're in no condition to be walking or taking buses. Second and Seventy-eighth, isn't it?" Mother Joseph would be doubly unhappy if the girl got away before they knew where to find her again.

Rose began to struggle. The sisters had no qualms about subtle coercion, but they drew the line at overt restraint. Sister Theresa's arm fell away.

"Don't be a stranger," she said, staring into Rose's haunted, gray eyes. "We care about you. We want to know how you're doing. We want to *help*. Come back and talk to us, Rose. Open your heart, then you'll truly feel better."

Rose looked at the ground, but her feet did not move. Sister Theresa knew it was time to set the hook.

"Saturday. Come for dinner. Roast chicken with corn-apple stuffing—just the way you always liked it . . ."

Eyelashes fluttered, but there was no answer.

"Say yes, dear. Make us all happy—"

Rose said yes without lifting her eyes from the ground, then she bolted. Her footfalls echoed on the chapel floor. She struck the fire bar on the outer door without pausing. They heard her race down the steps, then the door shut and she was gone. The chirping of the sparrows was the loudest sound until Mother Joseph found her voice.

"There's something seriously wrong there."

"But what?" Sister Agnes asked. "She's not ready to tell us or God. Should we follow her? Should we try to keep her here?"

"We've done all we can. Maybe she'll come Saturday. Maybe she'll tell us then."

"We should have kept her here," Sister Theresa grumbled. "*I* shouldn't have let her go."

"No," Mother Joseph admonished. She felt the same compassion the others did, but she answered to the city bureaucracy as well as to God and the diocese. Her options were limited. "We can do nothing against her will, not even for the good of her soul. We will pray that she comes on Saturday."

Another nun entered the discussion. "Did you see her look at that cat? I haven't seen a look like that except in the movies."

Mother Joseph adjusted the starched wimple beneath her veil, snatching an extra moment to consider what had been said. Cats had special privileges at the mission. They found sanctuary in every nook and cranny. Food and water were laid out for them each day. Sister Magdalene, who'd begun the tradition, wasn't here any longer. The Order was an army. The sisters went where they were told—although Mother Joseph had had a hand in getting Sister Magdalene out of Gotham City. But the cats continued to gather at the kitchen door and, from time to time, an envelope would appear in the poor box filled with untraceable currency. Mother Joseph understood that the money was for the cats.

"Perhaps we could invite another old friend to dinner on Saturday," Mother Joseph mused. "We haven't seen Selina in a while. Beelzebub's people-shy, but if Selina brought one of her kittens—she's always got a kitten or two—maybe we could get to the bottom of this."

"We haven't seen Selina since her sis—since Sister Magdalene left," Sister Theresa corrected herself quickly.

"I don't think they parted on . . ." She paused, choosing her words carefully. The stories about Sister Magdalene and her sister, Selina, were long, complex, and seldom told. ". . . in good faith with each other. I don't think Selina's even in the city anymore. And I don't think any good would come from getting her and Rose in the same room."

A murmur of agreement rippled through the black-robed flock that Mother Joseph squelched immediately. "*I* would like to know why Rose was frightened by a cat. And I'd like to invite Selina—to see if she'll come. Maybe she won't, and maybe nothing will happen if she does. But I want to see for myself. An unreasoning fear of cats has become much more widespread in Gotham City of late."

CHAPTER Five

*T*HE gray tiger kitten watched the box-thing follow him into the hiding room. At first it was very high, then it was level on the floor. Then it changed shape, and wonders began to erupt from it—an amazement of smells, sights, and sounds tumbling across the cold, hard floor. Curiosity seized him. It pulled him out of the safe place beneath the big hollow where water sometimes was and sometimes wasn't. Ears and tail twitching, stubby legs bunched beneath him, the kitten homed in on a fuzzy, wiggly, stringy thing. Wanting it more than anything else—needing it right now—he pounced.

"Gotcha!"

Hands descended without warning, pinching the skin above his shoulders, then raising him to dizzying heights.

"I knew you couldn't resist. No cat can resist a mess of sparkly junk."

The kitten found himself dangling in front of a face as large as himself. It wasn't the first time he'd been snatched from the brink of satisfaction. That face, the voice, and especially the hands were everywhere in his life. Usually they brought pleasure, but there was something different this time that made him wary.

"We've been invited to dinner. Both of us. The invitation was very specific: me and my most irresistible kitten. That's you. And since I make a habit of never refusing a free meal, you're going in the box."

The kitten hadn't understood a word, but he got the general idea. An instinctive expert in the squirming arts, he writhed until his claws hooked something solid, after which other instincts took over. A heartbeat later he was in free-fall.

"You drew blood!"

As nature intended, the kitten landed on his feet and scrabbling toward the door. The footing was lousy everywhere in his world. Slick bathroom tiles gave way to slick wood floors. He struck the door frame as he cornered and made more noise than forward progress down the hall.

"Get back here!"

Another thump against the door frame informed the kitten that the face and hands were on the move behind him. He bounded for the aptly named throw rug which spun him around the corner after which he made a flat-out dive for another safe place beneath the sleeping place. The other cats in the room—his littermates and a handful of adults—understood that chaos was near, and hastened its arrival by scrambling for shelter themselves.

Cats, knickknacks, newspapers, and the ruins of last night's dinner became airborne.

Selina Kyle had no time for conscious decision-making. She lunged for the nearest flying object, caught a gooey handful of cold Szechuan chicken, and watched with horror as a Ming-dynasty porcelain cat smashed against the wall.

"I liked that," she complained. "It was my favorite cat—"

Feline heads swiveled and stared with evident disbelief.

"I could've gotten three hundred for it, so it must've been worth thousands. But I didn't sell it. I took it because I liked it and I kept it because I liked it, and now it's *garbage*."

The cats blinked. One began grooming. Selina snatched a piece of drifted newspaper and cleaned the unappetizing veggies from her hand. The sauce was cold, but the spices still packed a wallop when she swiped them across the scratch the kitten left on her wrist. Once again her reflexes were faster than her thoughts. She had the stinging flesh pressed against her lips before she realized what she'd done, before the blob of paper and sauce ended its slide down the back of the sofa.

"Damn."

An orange tabby jumped down from a nearly empty bookshelf. It investigated the stain and withdrew, hissing.

"Double-damn."

Selina's one-room apartment wasn't large enough for seven—this afternoon—cats and one cat-loving human. She grabbed the newspaper and lobbed it toward the trash can. Her aim was solid, but the canister was already overflowing. The wad bounced to the floor. With a disgusted sigh, Selina packed the soggy newspaper into the canister and scuffed the porcelain bits in the general direction of the radiator. There was a broom somewhere, and roll of liners for the canister, but she didn't feel like looking for them.

She tried. At least once a month Selina made an effort to create the sort of home she supposed other people had, but she didn't have a gift for domesticity. She had other gifts. A gift for getting into things and out of them, for taking what she needed, for thriving where others might barely survive.

Her home looked like what it was: a scavenger's sanctuary. Some of it had been stolen, some rescued from dumpsters, most of it bought from thrift shops and sidewalk vendors. Selina gathered the things she thought belonged in a home—not the home she remembered, but a never-never home where everything was bright, glittering, and safe.

Selina took a deep breath as her possessions worked their magic. She hugged herself, swaying gently. Tensions drained down her back, through the floor, out of her life. Street sounds and building sounds pierced the walls—they always did in the East End—but the apartment itself was purring and peaceful.

The gray tiger kitten poked his head out and sneezed.

Selina triangulated the sound. ''There you are! You haven't won yet. Not hardly you haven't. I'm still getting my free meal, and you—you little devil—are still coming with me.''

Four-pawed backpedaling was a skill the kitten hadn't quite mastered. The hands followed him into the safe place. He spread his claws into the soft stuff beneath him, but the hands just dragged him and it into the light. He folded his ears against his head as a hand unhooked his claws one by one.

''No putting holes in the costume.'' Selina tapped the kitten on his nose, letting the length of supple leather fall. ''I share everything else, but that's *mine*.'' She scowled melodramatically at range two inches, and the kitten cringed.

Ignoring his wails, Selina put him in the box and closed it. A paw thrust through the cracks, slashing viciously. When that failed, Selina heard him attack the corrugated cardboard. Guessing that she had about a half hour before he escaped, Selina turned her attention to getting herself ready for a free dinner at the mission.

Selina was most comfortable in the costume draped across the unmade bed. Sheathed in black, hidden behind a mask, and defended by a set of razor-edged steel claws mounted in metal caps that were, themselves, somehow built into the costume's gloves, Selina ceased to be Selina. She became Catwoman. Viewed through a mask's eyeholes, the world was simple. Past and future were unimportant compared to the wants and needs of the present. The risks were great. Selina needed only to glance at the kitten's arm stretching desperately through the cardboard to understand how great.

Catwoman had her wits, her agility, her pride, and her determination—nothing more. She lived for herself, by herself, without illusions.

Having no illusions meant, at the very least, that the costume went back under the bed. If she wanted that free meal, she'd have to face the sisters as herself. Standing in her underwear before the haphazard piles spilling out of the closet and bureau, Selina heard a stern chorus from the depths of her past.

Look at yourself . . . Stand up straight. Don't fidget. Dress

*like a lady. Act like a lady. You're not leaving this house
dressed like that. You're cheap, Selina Kyle. You'll get in
trouble. You'll get what you deserve. Bitch. Whore. You'll
wind up in a gutter. Do you hear me, Selina Kyle? Look at
me when I'm talking to you!*

Selina braced for the clout she remembered much too well.
In the silent safety of her home she flinched, then stiffened
and smoldered.

"It isn't worth it," she murmured to the cats. "No meal's
worth this much remembering. I should've slammed that door
right in that nun's face."

But Selina had given her word. She donned whatever lay
at the top of the heaps: shapeless pants and a slouchy sweater,
a tattered photographer's vest, and military surplus boots.

"You may not look like a lady," she informed her reflection. "But you sure don't look like a whore."

Mother Joseph was waiting at the mission door. "Come
in, Selina. I'd begun to think you wouldn't keep your word.
Rose just got here." She reached for the box, from which
scratching and mewing could be heard. "And you brought
the kitten."

Selina eluded the nun's hands as she might dodge a knife
in a dark alley. *Trust a penguin to greet you with guilt,* she
thought to herself while curiosity about the other guest
swelled in the wordless part of her mind.

"Aggie-Pat didn't mention anyone else," she blurted out.
All the nuns had street names. Sister Theresa Carmel had
been TeeCee longer than anyone remembered. Sister Agnes
Patricia was Aggie-Pat; her real-life sister, Sister Margaret
Catherine was, naturally, Maggie-Cat. And Mother Joseph
was known throughout the East End as Old MoJo. But not
inside the mission. Selina didn't know why she'd used a street
name; she guessed it had something to do with feeling like a
kid and feeling angry at the same time.

Mother Joseph's expression didn't change. "Sister Agnes
was asked to invite you, not read you a guest list. You do
have a kitten in that box, don't you?"

Selina nodded, but held the box tight when Mother Joseph tried again to take it from her. "Why'd you want me to bring a kitten, anyway?"

Glancing back at the inner door through which other voices could be half heard, and sensing that Selina would not cooperate until she was more fully informed, Mother Joseph relented and pointed at the main stairway.

"Let's go to my office, Selina. I'll explain up there."

The satisfaction of being treated—for once—like an adult was almost enough to cancel the anxiety following Mother Joseph up the two flights to her office produced. It had been years since Selina had needed the mission's help. She'd paid everything back, with interest; she owed them nothing—but her heart started pounding anyway. When you came inside the mission, you accepted their rules. When you went upstairs it meant you'd broken some of those rules.

Good, bad, or indifferent, Selina didn't like rules, period. They made her a bit crazy. They made her Catwoman.

She was ready to explode when Mother Joseph unlocked the door and asked her to sit in one of the uncomfortable guest chairs. She got bored almost as soon as the nun opened her mouth. Selina lived in the East End, but Selina wasn't really a part of the East End community. She hadn't been born here. She hadn't set foot in Gotham until two weeks after her sixteenth birthday. Rose D'Onofreo's name wasn't familiar, nor were any of the others Mother Joseph prattled on about. The boredom began to show.

"Sometimes we use dolls to get the really troubled ones talking," Mother Joseph concluded hastily. "But with Rose, I think a cat will unlock her tongue—" She smiled at her own mild witticism. The smile vanished when Selina did not react. "Well, if you'll give Rose the box when we go downstairs—"

"There's a dinner in this eventually, isn't there? Roast chicken, dressing—the works, right?"

Mother Joseph rose from her chair. "Apple pie and vanilla ice cream for dessert, exactly as promised."

Aware that the nun was annoyed, but unable to pinpoint

the cause, Selina followed her meekly down the stairs. When the mission stuck to saving bodies, Selina had no trouble with them. Hot meals, clean sheets, showers, and the walk-in clinic were things everybody in this neighborhood needed from time to time. But saving souls, whether with religion or psychology, was a big waste of time. If this Rose person didn't have what it took to survive . . . If, God help her, she needed a *kitten*!

"Did you say something?" Mother Joseph asked. They were at the bottom of the stairway.

Selina slumped her shoulders. "Nope." Nuns were sharp enough to hear a person's thoughts, but they weren't sharp enough to know their softheaded idea of help was worse than no help at all.

Picking Rose out from the other women in the old-fashioned kitchen was easy: she was the only one not wearing a veil. As soon as she saw the long blond hair, Selina realized she did know Rose D'Onofreo—or know *of* her. When sleek limousines with dark windows came cruising the East End streets after midnight, they were looking for hair like that. Rose might have been born in a tenement bathroom, but she had uptown looks.

Not that they'd done her any good. Selina appraised the bruises on Rose's face with professional detachment. She took note of the wild-animal look in her eyes, too. A year— maybe less if the winter was bad—and that hair would be snarling in a refrigerator drawer down at the morgue.

"Hi," Rose said without making eye contact. "You're Selina Kyle, aren't you? You're Sister Magdalene's sister. I knew her when I was here. She was real—"

That was the last straw. Selina did *not* talk about Maggie, and these nuns knew damn well why. Her appetite was completely gone and the walls were closing in. Selina would have made a run for it, but Old MoJo was blocking the way.

"Yeah. She and I don't stay in touch."

Holding the kitten's box in front of her like a shield, Selina strode across the kitchen, defying anyone to mention Maggie's name again.

"I brought you something. . . . *Their* idea."

Selina didn't own any of the cats that shared her life. She didn't name them unless they forced her to. The kitten in the box was cute and bold, but that wasn't enough to give him a name. Rose could name him, if she wanted. Rose could do whatever she wanted. Selina told herself she didn't care, and that she could leave, but she didn't. She retreated a half-step and watched, just like everyone else.

The frightened look faded from Rose's eyes as she wrestled with the cardboard flaps. Selina expected the little tiger head to pop up as soon as the box was open. She expected Rose to melt completely in the face of its juvenile charm. Neither happened. The kitten hissed. Rose's hands flew away from the cardboard as if it had become searing hot.

A shiver raced down Selina's spine. It was the same shiver as when she pulled the costume over her arms and legs. She was uncannily alert without knowing why. Then she got a look at Rose's face. Costumed as Catwoman, Selina stalked in an unsuspecting city, but she was a thief, not a predator. Catwoman stole, and although she had killed, it was never personal. She'd never put death on someone's face the way the gray kitten put it on Rose's.

While Selina's heart thumped against her ribs, the battered blond woman saw death, feared it, accepted it, and finally invited it. Selina was forcing her heart to beat normally again when the kitten—the little gray tiger kitten who'd been captured, imprisoned, and jostled beyond his feline comprehension—succumbed to his instincts. He sprang at those wide-open eyes above him.

If he'd been a gray tiger, or even a tiger kitten, there surely would have been blood and blindness in the mission. Instead the kitten went flying as Rose let out a shriek that stunned all the other women, leaving them witless while she tumbled out of her chair. Rose tried to escape, but her arms and legs would not behave. Her flailing movements, the peculiar breathy sounds she made after she stopped shrieking awoke primitive resonances:

Flee. Death comes, all-mighty and inevitable. Flee. Don't

think. Don't look back. The beast of death is feeding.
Flee, if you fear the beast. Flee, if you would see the sun
again.

It took a special kind of stupid—not just human stupid,
but civilized human stupid—to disobey that primal voice.
Mother Joseph was the first to disobey. She shook off her
deepest instincts with a shudder, then she was kneeling on
the floor, giving orders to the others as she struggled to keep
Rose from crawling under the sink.

Selina was the last to recover. The huddling nuns, Rose's
mottled, terrified face—none of this was part of Selina's
world. She saw the cardboard box on its side. She looked for
the kitten and found him, fluffed out and panting, as far from
Rose as the room allowed him to get. She gathered him
against her breast. The beating of her heart calmed him.

"It's not your fault," she whispered. "It's not your fault."

Selina stayed in the shadows beside the wall until the kitten
emitted a blissed-out purr and made cat-fists in her sweater.
She endured the prickly claws until Catwoman's hyperalert-
ness had subsided and she was her ordinary self again.

The sisters, led by Mother Joseph, were determined to find
evidence of the drugs they blindly believed were the root of
Rose's problems. Selina started to tell them that they were
wasting their time, but thought against it before they'd noticed
her. Old MoJo's reaction was understandable. Drugs usually
were the cause of everything here in the East End—especially
if alcohol was counted as a drug and growing up surrounded
by it was called drug abuse. By that standard, drugs were to
blame not only for Rose, but for Selina herself.

Getting a firm grip on the kitten, Selina headed for home.

You had to draw the line somewhere. If you accepted that
you were a victim, you stayed a victim. Somewhere you had
to stop being a victim. You didn't have to become a wild-
eyed crusader; you just had to stop being anybody's victim,
ever again. Batman was a crusader; whoever Batman was
behind his mask, he had been a victim. Of what, when,
or why Selina couldn't guess, but she was certain of her
conclusions.

"Takes one to know one," she said aloud, surprising herself and the wino in a darkened doorway.

"You tell 'em, sister. Got any change? A smoke? A light?"

One-handedly buttoning her raincoat and hunching her shoulders around the kitten, Selina kept going. She didn't like being on the streets after dark—at least not without the costume. It was altogether too easy to become a victim.

Like Rose.

She was thinking about Rose and victims when she came in sight of a clutch of youths. They'd staked a claim to a lamppost with macho posturing and a pumping boombox. The kitten struggled; Selina needed both hands to confine him. The motion—pressing both hands against her breasts—drew unwanted attention.

Selina saw herself with their eyes: a woman, alone, wringing her hands with terror. It didn't matter whether she was hideous or attractive. It didn't matter that she was the master of kinds of martial arts that won fights, not exhibitions. For an instant Selina felt the look she'd seen in Rose's eyes.

They whistled and propositioned her lewdly. One of the punks swaggered onto the street.

"You wanna dance?" He stood with his feet apart, hips slightly forward, and the bill of his baseball cap shielding his eyes. "C'mon, bitch." He took his hands out of his pockets. "You gonna get it whether you want it or not."

Everything conspired against her, from the squirming kitten to the clothes she was wearing. She didn't look like Catwoman; she didn't feel like Catwoman. And the punk was moving closer. Then a finger of ice skipped down her spine. Her gut shrank and the fear turned to rage.

"Not on your best day." The words didn't matter. Everything depended on the edge of her voice and the thrust of her glare through shadow to the place where his eyes had to be. "Not with all your slime friends helping you." Selina forgot where they were, what she held, and even who she was. She forgot that the costume was stuffed under the bed. Her rage spread across her face. Like a giant spark it leapt between her eyes and his.

She had him.

"You one crazy bitch," the punk murmured, retreating.

Selina ached to see his eyes, to hear his voice when his mouth was full of broken teeth and blood. Not this time. The kitten still squirmed. She'd have to be content with breaking his spirit for a few hours, and the hope that his peers by the lamppost would sense his injury and finish the job for her.

"Beat it, slime, while you still can."

He tugged on the bill of his cap. Maybe he thought he'd regain the advantage if he met the crazy lady's eyes. If he had, he was wrong. Selina was waiting for him. She showed real teeth through a real smile and started toward him, then walked on by. As she had hoped, his erstwhile companions hurled insults until she was out of earshot.

Another hundred yards and she began to relax.

Only a man can make a woman forget everything but fear.

The thought spread through her mind along with Rose's face. The punk's eyes were astonished. Like the druggers, he couldn't quite believe that a woman—a bitch—had overwhelmed him. But there was no astonishment, surprise, or disbelief in the memory of Rose's face, only fear, then a victim's acceptance of inevitable fate.

CHAPTER
Six

SELINA let herself into her apartment. The kitten escaped before she got the door shoved shut. The locks reset automatically.

A case of tuna fish was stacked in the kitchen cabinets. As easy to prepare and serve as it was to store, tuna was one of Mother Nature's almost-perfect foods—especially when each can was certified dolphin-safe. She opened a can and, leaning over the sink, began eating the contents with her fingers.

Her hunger knots loosened; her thoughts wandered back to the mission. Selina was angry at Old MoJo and the others. They'd used her, they'd used the kitten, and they'd cheated her out of a meal. It was a superficial anger, though, and would be gone before the tuna can was empty. There was a deeper layer of anger, though, that was not so easily erased. The world was full of people who didn't like cats. Dislike could turn to hatred, but, in adults, it rarely showed itself as stark fear. Rose's fear of cats wasn't something she'd carried around since childhood.

Licking tuna slivers from her fingers, Selina set the almost-empty can on the floor for the cats to scour.

There was only one conclusion that felt right: There was a

man behind Rose's terror, but somehow he'd managed to displace her fear from him to an innocent cat.

Selina held her breath as a familiar but not quite comfortable sensation passed over her. She let her breath out raggedly. The transformation from her ordinary self to Catwoman was complete before Selina left the alcove that her landlord called a kitchen. She shed clothes with every step toward the bed and was nearly naked by the time she reached it. The sleek costume fit like a second skin—as well it should. The garment had been obscenely expensive.

In the beginning she tried using secondhand costumes from theatrical supply houses. She'd even tried making one herself. Nothing stood up to the punishment her alter ego gave it. Then one day a clumsily written letter slid under the door. The outside hall was eerily empty. The paper bore a sketch, a price, and an address where the transaction could be completed. It scared Selina witless, but she was ready to try anything. She assembled the asking price in gold and other specified substances, left it on a bench in a deserted courtyard, and found the leather costume laid across her bed one evening two weeks later.

As she smoothed the costume over her arms and legs, Selina Kyle vanished. The simpler Catwoman stood in her place.

"I'll be back before dawn," she whispered to the assembled pairs of glowing eyes. "Don't wait up." She eased along the ledge, around the corner, and was gone.

Between the tuna fish and the costume, Selina had considered other ways of resolving her curiosity. She briefly pictured herself at the mission. The doors of the mission were never closed, but the nuns weren't foolish enough to stay downstairs after dark. If Selina went there now, she'd have to explain herself to the brawny ex-addicts who ran the night shelter like a marine boot camp. Not likely. She thought of telephoning Mother Joseph directly, but Old MoJo wouldn't be in her office taking calls at this hour. Besides, Selina's phone wasn't working . . . again. One of the cats—she didn't know which—had developed a taste for plastic wire insulation. It probably wasn't good for the cat, but it was fatal for the phone.

And if Selina had spoken to Mother Joseph, what then? If Old MoJo had known anything useful about Rose, would she have invited Selina to bring a kitten to dinner? For all that the nuns had been in the East End much longer than Selina herself, they were women who had chosen to live without men. What did any of them know about the real world—the man-dominated world where Selina and Rose lived?

Catwoman landed between the carved stone gargoyles overlooking the mission. Her body flexed from toes to neck, absorbing the impact, keeping her balanced for whatever the next moment required. Crouched in the shadows, she listened to the city noises, straining to hear anything that meant she had been spotted jumping from the tenement to the church roof. She could have been spotted and she could have been heard. Whatever else the Catwoman was, she was not endowed with uncanny powers, but most people had no notion of the untapped potential within their bodies.

Gotham was never quiet. At best the auditory chaos ebbed to an ignorable drone from which the alert ear could always discern sirens, screams, and the occasional gunshot—four of them, small-calibre semiautomatic over by the docks. Catwoman's lips parted in an unconscious snarl. With her mind's eye she could see the lightweight, lethal, and almost certainly foreign-made weapon. She knew the hardware by sight and sound, though she shunned it personally. She'd heard the old men—survivors from the sixties—mutter about the days of zip guns and Saturday night specials that were as likely to blow up in your face as take out the opposition. Those days were gone long before she got off the bus. Since the Gulf war, a Saturday night special was an army-surplus grenade.

Though the docks were a dozen blocks away, Catwoman listened for answering fire. She didn't expect to head that way before going home, but one never knew. A wise person, no matter where they were or how they were dressed, paid attention to night sounds. The next sound she heard was a police siren screaming down Ninth Avenue, going somewhere in a big hurry, but not to the docks.

Selina relaxed and lowered herself onto the mission roof. Her claws made short work of the skylight's security. She dropped into the stairwell, then froze and waited breathlessly. The noise had seemed horrendously loud in her own ears, but it raised no alarm.

Two hours later, after fruitlessly inspecting every nook and cranny into which a body could fit, Catwoman returned to the stairwell and sprang upward toward the open skylight. The molding sagged when her fingers clamped over it, but the old wood held and she pulled herself easily onto the deserted rooftop. Blending with the night sky and the satiny black of the asphalt roof, Selina pushed the mask back from her face. A gentle breeze, scented with salt from the riverfront, refreshed her as she considered her predicament.

Rose D'Onofreo wasn't inside the mission. Remembering how she'd tried to hide under the sink, it was hard to imagine that she'd recovered and gone home.

The warble of an ambulance—markedly different from the whoop or shriek of a squad car or the airhorn belch of fire equipment—echoed off the nearby buildings. Before coming to Gotham, Selina would count the seconds between the sight of lightning and the sound of thunder; now she listened to the changing pitch and guessed which of the huge hospitals was its destination. The siren faded straightaway; the vehicle hadn't turned toward Gotham General. It was going all the way downtown to the university medical center. Whoever was inside was in a world of hurt.

Could the nuns have sent Rose to Gotham General? The mission had its own infirmary. Selina had checked it out along with everything else and found it occupied by a noisy, but harmless, drunk. The sisters would have kept Rose in the infirmary unless they thought she'd die before Sunday morning, because on Saturday night there wasn't an emergency room in the city that had time or room for a *minor* emergency.

Selina pulled the hooded mask down over her face. Rather

than brood about where Rose might be, she'd let herself into
Old MoJo's office and find out for sure. Mother Joseph trusted
God, the holy saints, and no one else. The lock on her office
door was state of the art, but still no match for the supple
steel rods Catwoman extracted from an invisible pocket on
her thigh. She entered the office and closed the door silently
behind her. Her eyes were already adjusted to the darkness;
she could have held a phone book at arm's length and read
each number without strain.

The desk was messy—a good sign; it had been unnaturally
neat when she'd been here with the kitten earlier. With her
arms linked behind her back, Catwoman leaned over, studying the disorder without disturbing it.

"What the—?"

Old MoJo's handwriting was Parochial School Perfect.
Every word was legible; the problem was, most of them
weren't English. After a moment Selina decided they were
Latin.

"Not even the Pope uses Latin . . ."

But Latin it was, and remained, no matter how fiercely she
stared at it. Selina felt an urge to sweep everything onto the
floor, to smash and shatter all that could be broken. Her hands
slipped free, they hovered above the desk. It was urges like
this that had always gotten her into trouble. Slowly she knotted her fingers, pressing the steel claws harmlessly into the
black leather sewn across her palms.

"Easy," Catwoman whispered. "Just because Old MoJo
writes some dumb, dead language doesn't mean you can't
figure out what she did with Rose."

There was a phone on Mother Joseph's desk: a sleek
techno-toy with a wide variety of buttons and a single flashing
red light.

"Be calm. Think. *Think*."

A steel claw caressed the button nearest the flashing light.

"Hello? Hello? This is Dr. Gallan's service. If you're
there, Sister, pick up." The nasal, feminine voice paused
dramatically. "Dr. Gallan wants you to know that she got
your message and is on her way. I want to know where she's

going. She didn't have the number. She said we could get it from you. So call us," and the woman recited the number.

Catwoman smiled, memorizing it while the machine reset itself. Then she lifted the handset and pressed another button. A rapid, ten-note melody played in her ear. Selina wasn't a musical genius. She didn't have perfect pitch and she'd have to press the redial button many more times before she could memorize the melody, but she knew she hadn't made a local call and she was pretty sure she hadn't called Dr. Gallan's service.

The circuit closed. Somewhere a phone rang once, twice . . . a dozen times. Catwoman was about to give up when the handset came to life.

"Eye-aitch-em, Martyr's Blood."

Catwoman was nonplussed by the cryptic greeting. Fortunately, the groggy woman at the other end of the line blamed herself for the silence and tried again:

"Sisters of the Immaculate Heart, Blood of Holy Martyr's Convent, Mother House. May I help you?"

"I hope so," the black-costumed woman replied. It all made sense once she remembered that religious orders had a quasimilitary organization. The sisters here were soldiers of the Immaculate Heart army; Old MoJo was their commanding officer; the East End mission was a front-line outpost. And Blood of Holy Martyr's Convent wasn't just another fort, it was their army headquarters. "I'm trying to locate Rose D'Onofreo."

"Rose D'Onofreo . . . ? I don't know . . ."

The woman didn't sound uncertain, she sounded suspicious. Catwoman changed tactics. "I'm sorry. The person I'm really looking for is Dr. Gallan. This is her service. We seem to have lost track of her. The last we knew she was seeing a Rose D'Onofreo at this number."

"Dr. Gallan? Yes, she was here, but she left hours ago. I don't know who . . . No, wait, it was a young woman from the mission." Time expired as the convent woman became fully awake. "Who is this? Where are you calling from? Why are you asking about Rose—"

Catwoman reached down and severed the connection with a claw. With the help of a picture a few inches from the phone, she'd learned all she needed to know. The snapshot showed the smiling faces of a quartet of nuns Selina didn't recognize. That didn't matter. What mattered was the mansion behind them and the sign beside them. The words were a bit hard to read—Old MoJo needed a lesson on focusing her camera—but at least they were in English: Sister Servants of the Immaculate Heart of Mary. Blood of the Holy Martyr's Convent. Mother House. And an address so complete it included the zip code and the phone number.

Rose was safe inside the Mother House. Whatever had terrorized her wouldn't dare penetrate those walls. But Catwoman would have to, if Selina wanted to know anything more.

At that moment, Selina wanted only to go home.

She climbed her building's fire escape, then vaulted over the wrought-iron railing and eased along the masonry ledge. The cats came and went through the window grate. Catwoman went that way, but she came back through a corner window after checking the home out in a discreetly mounted mirror. A costume and its reputation were no guarantee against surprises.

Selina shed the costume immediately, returning it to its place beneath the bed with a casual kick. Her conscience, speaking with her mother's voice, warned her to treat it better. She ignored the warning, as she ignored most of the well-intended and occasionally wise advice that dead woman had given her.

Without turning on the lights, she showered and cleared a space for herself amid the cats on the rumpled bed. The gray tiger kitten was curled up on the only pillow. He hissed when she slid her hand beneath him and dug in with his claws. She hissed right back and dumped him on the floor. She was asleep before he was back snuggling into the curve of her neck.

Selina Kyle didn't dream. Dreams were for other people. She had nightmares, but she learned to stop remembering them years ago. So Selina didn't dream about Rose and she didn't dream that the little gray kitten had turned into a snarling beast. She didn't remember being Rose, or becoming the beast. She didn't shiver with fear, or sweat with rage, but when she woke up with the midday sun burning her eyes, Selina felt as if she'd been on the losing side of a prolonged war. She tried to get on track with exercise.

Cats that were born cats didn't have to exercise; they slept, ate, groomed, hunted, or played—mostly slept. Catwoman was human, and she needed exercise, a lot of it, to keep her reflexes sharp and her muscles toned. She exercised at least four hours every day. Sometimes it was all she did besides sleeping and eating. She wasn't into grooming or playing.

This morning, though, Selina's arms were spaghetti and her feet were lead. Her legs got tangled up in the jump rope; she bloodied her lip crashing to the floor. Then she lost her balance doing handstand push-ups and flopped on her back like a sack of cement. The cats gathered around, exchanging wise glances. When the gray kitten clawed his way up her shoulder and stood with his forepaws on her chin, staring into her left eye, she admitted defeat.

Catwoman would have to find the Bloody Martyr's convent if Selina wasn't going to start remembering her dreams again. But first Selina would have to find out where Riverwyck was, and how to get there. Catwoman's knowledge of Gotham ended at the city limits. She never took vacations and didn't even have a driver's license. It took until Tuesday to figure out where the bedroom community was located and which train line went there, because an ongoing budget crisis kept the public libraries closed on Sunday and Monday. She wound up buying a round-trip ticket and waiting impatiently amid a throng of suits and briefcases for the afternoon exodus express. The businesswomen simply pretended she wasn't there. The men appraised her East End wardrobe (boldly patterned leggings, neon green V-neck sweater, door-knocker earrings—it had seemed reasonable enough downtown) and smirked or looked away. One of them had the gall to ask if she'd be available later on, say, after ten? The would-be philanderer scuttled away as soon as Selina focused her cold, glassy stare on him.

She shouldered her way onto the train ahead of the regulars. She chose a window seat for herself and the aisle seat beside it for the backpack containing the costume. A handful of commuters were still standing when the train pulled out of the station. No one laid a hand on the pack or suggested she remove it. Her obsidian aura remained unchallenged until she'd hiked a mile beyond the Riverwyck station, when, without warning, she was bathed from behind with glaring white and crimson lights.

Cops.

Selina didn't need Catwoman's help to deal with cops; she'd been hustling the law before she got to Gotham City.

"Where you headed, miss?" The officer emerging from the passenger side looked young enough to do undercover work in an elementary school. He reeked of college and too many sensitivity-training courses. "We don't see many strangers walking down this road. We thought you might be lost."

He said it so sincerely that Selina almost believed him— almost didn't know what to say—then she got a look at the other standard-issue cop taking up space behind the steering wheel. Cops were cops. The only difference was that these two would probably fall for a line that wouldn't fool an East End rookie.

"I'm looking for the convent. I heard there was a convent around here. I thought, maybe, they'd be able to help. I've got a *problem*."

The college cop turned to his partner; he left his back wide open. A few moments later Selina was getting a ride the rest of the way—and she was glad of it. What had been two and a half inches on the map worked out to about ten cross-country miles.

Selina expected to have a close escort all the way to the Mother Superior, but the rubes let her out with smiles at the gate. She returned the smiles and, as soon as they were gone, hid behind some shrubbery to change into the costume.

Mother Joseph's photograph did not do justice to the vast estate. At night all the jumbled rooflines, Victorian turrets and towers left the place looking like a for-real fortress—and that was only the main building. Catwoman emerged from the bushes knowing that getting in would be the least of her troubles. Finding Rose could take a week of midnight explorations, unless she could improve the odds. She took the time to scout the estate thoroughly. After completing the circuit she went back to a separate guest-type house that had looked promising. There were grated windows on the second floor with no fire escapes to justify them.

Her hunch paid off. The second-story rooms were tiny, their doors had windows, and the security was meant to keep people in, not out. A night-duty nurse was watching television. She felt a draft and left her desk to check the stairwell door. It was in order, as was everything else she could see. She went back to her desk.

Catwoman found Rose in the second room she checked. The young woman lay on her back, looking like a peaceful corpse. Catwoman moved cautiously toward her.

"Rose?" Her voice was gentle, but her arms were tensed.

And it was a good thing that they were. Rose awakened with a jolt. She saw the dark silhouette coming at her and panicked. Belatedly Catwoman considered that her costume might not be a comforting sight. It was too late for reconsideration. The women wrestled. Catwoman won handily.

"I've come to help you," she said when she had one hand over Rose's mouth and the other pinning her firmly to the mattress. The terror in Rose's eyes intensified. "I won't hurt you." No indication of belief in the bulging eyes. "The cats didn't mean to hurt or frighten you. They sent me to say they're sorry and to make things right for you. But I can't do that unless you can answer my questions. Tell me his name. Tell me the name of the man who made you more afraid of cats than him."

A final surge of terror shook Rose's body, then she went limp. Catwoman removed her hands gingerly. Fear could do many strange things; it could kill. Rose's eyes fluttered. She took a deep breath and sat up slowly.

"Eddie. Eddie talks to the cats. They're everywhere. They're all dead, but they answer him. They make him strong and smart. Then he makes them watch me."

Catwoman shook her head. She was too late; Rose had gone around the bend. "Eddie who?" she asked, not knowing if she dared to believe any answer she got.

"*My* Eddie. Eddie Lobb." Rose hesitated. She looked past Catwoman to someone only she could see, or remember. "You know Eddie. He made good. He has his own business. He has nice things. He gave me things. Nice things when I worked for him. Then he said I should live with him. He said I was his woman. He had a place near the park. A nice place—except for the cats. Big cats. Lions, tigers, panthers—mostly tigers. Eyes everywhere, watching me. His place. A nice place. Him and the cats. All the cats. All watching me. Then he put them in the room with me." She began twisting the blankets into a tight spiral, then she began to gnaw on them.

Catwoman retreated until her back was against the wall.

"It watched me all the time. All the time. He told me that if I was good, it would make me strong the way the other tigers were making him strong. I wanted to be strong. I wanted to be good." She missed the blanket and drew blood from her knuckles. "I tried so hard, Eddie. I really did. I didn't mean to be bad. I can be good again. I promise. You don't have to hit me, Eddie. I love you, you know I do."

Catwoman bolted from the room, not caring what the night nurse saw or thought.

Mist was creeping around the convent walls when Catwoman reached the ground outside the grated windows. It changed to rain while she looked for a lair in which to spend the night. (There were no night trains going through Riverwyck. The community was a bedroom for Gotham, and the trains ran accordingly.) The costume could keep Catwoman dry in any weather, but it was better at keeping her cool when it was hot than keeping her warm when it was cold, damp, and miserable. She retrieved her backpack and started wandering among the outbuildings. When she found an unlocked toolshed, she slipped inside and made herself a bed in a pile of musty tarpaulins.

CHAPTER
Seven

*N*OT long after Selina closed her eyes, and not all that far away either, Bruce Wayne hunkered down in an ergonomically correct computer-user's chair that resembled the illegitimate offspring of a fold-down church kneeler and a bar stool. He squirmed constantly and unconsciously. After thirty-six hours staring at the monitor, crunching data, and surviving on black coffee and snacks Alfred managed to shove under his nose, his body had used up all its comfortable positions. A lesser man might have quit, taken a shower, gotten some sleep, and started again when the sun was shining and his mind was fresh.

Batman was not a lesser man.

Ranks and files of phosphorescent green marched up and off the screen. Bruce Wayne's hands were poised above the keyboard, ready to stop the flow. His eyes were unblinking. His pupils were wide and steady, absorbing the information rather than reading it. Wayne was dressed for comfort and endurance in dark, loose-fitting slacks and a cotton knit shirt. The Batman costume was in its locker at the back of the large, subterranean room they called the Batcave. In the dim light, his clothing blurred with the furniture and the gray stone walls.

Standing at the top of a flight of metal stairs, Alfred saw Bruce's hands, trembling with caffeine overload, and the flickering green light reflecting off his motionless face. The war paint of a technological primitive.

"I've brought a snack, sir."

No reaction. Alfred descended the steep stairway. He was no longer a young man, but his step was steady. Nothing on the silver tray shook or clattered to give his presence away. He set it on the top of a file cabinet, beside a similar tray bearing the unappetizing remains of an untouched dinner.

"Sir." Alfred found the tone midway between command and request that distinguished butlers from all other human subspecies. "Sir," he repeated, "this really has gone on long enough."

"I'm close, Alfred. I can feel it."

"You were 'close' this morning when I brought breakfast. By now 'close' is behind you."

Bruce Wayne surrendered his concentration with a groan. His hands fell on the keyboard; the marching figures halted. "I'm nailing jelly to a tree," he admitted, using hacker's jargon.

At times like this he was, essentially, a computer hacker. A technology wizard shining lights through the back doors of every major data bank in the world. Over the course of several long days, he'd extracted enough raw information to keep a hundred data-gnomes busy for a lifetime. Thirty-six hours ago he'd thrown it all into the cybernetic equivalent of a centrifuge. Since then he'd been spinning the data down through a bewildering series of customized algorithms. He was fully aware that his eyes were glazed and his mind was numb. It was at times like this—when his brain was reduced to its most primitive processes—that his mind was best attuned to subtle variations in pure pattern or rhythm. He was waiting for the neurons in his visual cortex to erupt and alert the rest of him to a deviation in the data flow.

"I've sorted it on every variable. Hit every correlation.

Nothing stands out. He's there—I know he is. These are his deals. I recognize them. I come so close, and then he's gone into a web of corporations and money transfers. He's tickled the Wayne Foundation more than once to clean up his profits. Never the same way twice, never overt. He does things in pieces that look harmless enough—''

Wayne's fingers clattered across the keyboard, bringing up a frozen section of prior data. After he tapped the screen with an optical stylus, a second window opened—the reincorporation papers of what appeared to be some sort of food-processing facility.

"Here's a little juice factory in Florida that was shut down after the mid-eighties freezes wiped out the orange groves. Suddenly it's got a contract to process second-rate apricots from California. Fifty honest people get jobs rendering bruised fruit into generic fruit syrup and by-products. What do you think happens next?''

Alfred pursed his lips. With a thirty-room mansion to care for, he almost always had better things to do than play guessing games. But the terms "second-rate" and "by-products" pointed him in a particular direction. "Someone puts the by-products into animal feed and people get sick?''

"The Connection's too crafty for that. In his deals—especially his American deals—everybody seems to come out ahead.'' He tapped the screen again. Now it showed a series of invoices. "Our reincorporated syrup-maker is concerned about the environment. It adds an extra step to its end-processing to concentrate toxins, extract them, seal them in fifty-gallon barrels which they ship to a brand-new company up in North Carolina, where skilled jobs are even more precious and people will welcome a hazardous-materials recycler with open arms.''

Another tap, another screen—a list of chemicals by common name, scientific name, and formula. One of the formulas was blinking. Alfred saw a (CN) notation in the middle of it.

"That's cyanide, isn't it?'' he asked soberly.

"Five barrels a month, extracted from apricot sludge in Florida. You can't recycle it, but you can sell it—and so they do. Here's a standing order for all our apricot residue. It's supposed to go to a chemical conglomerate in the unified Germany. I could find where the barrels get hoisted into a ship's hold, but, by the records, they never come off. Three or four tramp freighters show up regularly in Shreveport, Louisiana, to take on cargo. It seems safe to assume that they are empty when they arrive in Shreveport, but there's no sign that they've ever been off-loaded anywhere in the past two years."

"There must be an error somewhere, a gap in the paperwork—"

"More likely a quick coat of marine paint somewhere on the high seas. Ship A vanishes, but Ship B sails into port right on schedule."

"A very large gap in the paperwork," Alfred agreed.

"Ships arrive in ports like San'a in South Yemen where America doesn't have a consulate, and no one asks questions about where a few extra barrels are going, or where they've been."

"Where do they go from there?"

Bruce Wayne tapped the glass a final time. The display shrank into a single green dot, then the screen was blank. "Iran, Iraq, Syria—any place that might want to secretly develop a few chemical weapons to drop on their neighbors. The Connection's broken the laws of no single country. A couple hundred families here in the United States have food on their tables because of this, of him—and somewhere somebody's making chemical weapons."

Moments passed. The computer kept time, then activated a background program that began filling the screen with random blobs of primary colors. The effect momentarily mesmerized both men.

"And those other Arabs," Alfred began gently, "those Bess-arabs you were looking for—were you able to find them, at least?"

"Bessarabia, no Bessarabians. Somewhere around the Black Sea. It's a place like New England or the Rust Belt—

referenced by people who clearly believe it exists, but it doesn't show up on any maps. At least not any maps in here.'' Wayne thumped the console. The movement was enough to cause the screen to go blank again. ''It's been swapped back and forth between Russia and Rumania a couple of times just in this century.''

Alfred straightened. ''Does this mean that Commissioner Gordon has been misinformed by the international authorities?''

''The region was part of the Soviet Union. Nobody knows what's going on over there right now. The Communists hid everything beneath a thick coat of red paint, and now the paint's peeling. Most of our data is suspect, but at least we've got data. The Kremlin ran that country for seventy years on terror and rumor. Open the lid on the Soviet box and you're looking into the Dark Ages, not the twentieth century. But somebody lives in Bessarabia. Somebody got traded back and forth between governments like chips in a poker game. Somebody could be a terrorist—and if he is, the Connection would be right there to do business with him.''

''A shadow arms-merchant for a shadow terrorist. It does seem appropriate. What about that Tiger fellow? He sounded real enough.''

''Real enough, but not big enough. Gotham City records show him growing up right here—if growing up is the right word for it. The juvenile records are sealed, but there're quite a few of them. He got into a lot of fights. Wound up in the hospital as often as he popped up at the East End precinct. Then, about a dozen years ago he left town—headed south. He either stayed clean the ten years he was gone, or he got in trouble somewhere that still has all their records in a dusty file cabinet. These days he runs an import-export business from the old neighborhood. The police keep a close eye on him. They know he's trouble, but they can't prove it.''

''Does he work for the Connection?''

''He does some work for the Connection,'' Batman corrected. ''But, then again, according to what I've learned, so has the Wayne foundation. I'll trail him, work my way up the ladder, but Gordon set a time limit. I don't see Tiger yielding fruit quickly enough.''

"Then what?''

"I'll keep looking for these Connection transactions and hope I get lucky, hope I find something floating in the Black Sea.''

Wayne hammered a lengthy keystroke command and the phosphorescent green army began marching up the screen again. He hunched forward, the glaze formed on his eyes again.

Alfred found his butler's voice. "Forgive me for saying this, sir—but it seems to me that if you're looking for this Bessarabia, you're not going to find it in a computer. You'd do better looking in a book. Have you considered going upstairs and using the library?''

Bruce Wayne hadn't. He lowered his hands to the keyboard, stopping the data march, while his fatigued mind summoned all the reasons books were inferior to sophisticated data-processing techniques—provided, of course, that the data existed in processible form. And in the matter of Bessarabia, it did not. Muttering under his breath about the fallacies of communism, Bruce Wayne prepared to disentangle himself from his ergonomic seat. His knees were numb, his ankles unresponsive; he lurched forward, catching his balance for a moment with his knuckles and spreading such handwritten notes as he'd made in the last five days across the console table.

"Harry Mattheson?'' Alfred inquired, spotting the words in bold isolation on an otherwise blank sheet. "Where did his name come from?''

Scowling, Batman collected the papers in a neat pile. Harry's name disappeared. "His name popped out in the early going, before I got the search parameters refined.''

"You were looking for the Connection and Harry's name popped up?''

Bruce raked his wilted hair off his forehead. He evaded Alfred's raised eyebrows and took a stride toward the stairs.

"Did it?"

"I was asking the wrong questions. My own name popped up, too, as President of the Wayne Foundation. I didn't write it down."

"But you wrote down Harry's name."

With a weary, irritated sigh, Wayne confronted the only man alive who could challenge him this way. "Harry Mattheson was one of my father's closest friends. They served together overseas, and after the war they helped each other out. He sits on the board of the Wayne Foundation, for heaven's sake. We don't see eye to eye on many things, but I've known him my whole life. I might as well suspect myself as Harry."

Blessed with a butler's logic and a recent night's sleep, Alfred was tempted to say that Bruce Wayne, who led a double life as Batman, was indeed a perfect suspect—and so was Harry. He resisted the temptation, however, since his goal was to get Bruce moving toward his bedroom and that goal had almost been accomplished. After he slept, Bruce would find the error in his logic without any assistance, and he would be refreshed enough to make good use of it.

But things did not go Alfred's way. Bruce paused partway up the stairs. He cocked his head, and from his place beside the console, the butler could fairly see the fog lifting from his friend's shoulders and logic falling heavily into place. He drew an imperceptible breath and hoped Bruce would continue up the stairs.

"You're right, Alfred. I would suspect myself. To acquire what Batman needs, I've had to cast a web of international and financial confusion. I've got the contacts. I've got the computers, the money, the network of holding companies— all so no one could do what I do and connect me with Batman. The motive is different—entirely different—but I *could* be the Connection."

Alfred combined the items on the two silver trays and prepared to follow Bruce up the stairs. "Might I remind you," he said almost reluctantly, "that the Mattheson fortune grew out of Blue Star Shipping Lines?"

"He shut that down." Wayne's voice wandered.

"Maybe he just gave the Blue Star ships a new coat of marine paint. . . ."

The steel railing vibrated from the intensity of Batman's grip. "Harry. But why? Why—?" He looked across the cave chamber at the bank of digital clocks on the back wall. It was just after one A.M. "Alfred—I'm going to my club."

"But, sir . . ."

"I look like death—I know. Bruce Wayne hasn't gone to his club in weeks. Showing up looking like I do right now—or a little worse—will feed everyone's worst suspicions. Harry Mattheson has never failed to call me out to lunch for a fatherly lecture whenever he thinks I'm letting the Wayne foundation—and my father's memory—down. Well, I'm more than ready to do lunch with Uncle Harry."

"You have no idea if he's even in town. Please, sir, there must be a better way." Generations of understairs expertise shaped the butler's inflection; Queen Victoria herself would have reconsidered.

But not Batman.

"I'll make an entrance that he's sure to hear about. Bruce Wayne: the debaucher debauched; scoundrel and squanderer. Maybe I'll even make the papers, Alfred. It's been a while since Bruce Wayne has tromped across the gossip pages." He released the railing and charged up the stairs two at a time.

Alfred started up the stairs at a more reasoned pace. "I'll await you in the car, sir."

There was always a chance that Bruce would see his reflection in the mirror and realize this was no time for playacting, but it was a slim chance and Alfred wasted no time getting down to the garage. He guided the limousine out of its stall, parking it conveniently close to the door and coincidentally blocking the sports car. Bruce Wayne stood in the doorway. He surveyed Alfred's careful arrangement and accepted it without comment.

If he had not known the precise condition of every garment in Bruce's wardrobe, Alfred might have believed that he'd found his tuxedo rolled up in a ball behind a door somewhere. It was criminally wrinkled. The cummerbund and tie were both slightly askew and there was a reddish smear on the starched white shirt that could pass for wine, lipstick, or blood—depending on the prejudice of the observer. He landed on the leather seat with a thud that shook the car's suspension.

"Drive on, my good man," Bruce said jocosely. "To the club."

Alfred knew better than to say anything. The real Bruce Wayne—to the extent that there was a real Bruce Wayne—was gone, replaced by a sotted, irresponsible playboy. He pushed the button to raise the smoked-glass partition, and a second button to turn the heat on. Perhaps a forty-five-minute ride in the back of a stuffy limousine would accomplish what reason could not, but, no—several customized lights on the dashboard flickered to life. Bruce had activated the remote computer and was recalibrating his data searches at a furious rate.

The electronic gate swung open to let the limo out of the estate, then swung and locked shut behind them. Alfred guided the car down the dark, deserted rural road toward the always-visible amber dome of Gotham-by-night. Less than an hour later he jockeyed the lumbering vehicle into line outside a seemingly deserted office tower.

Bruce Wayne's club was at the top of the tower—a quietly expensive amalgam of antique and modern that made the statement: the best of everything never clashes with itself. The same could be said for the men who sat in air-conditioned comfort before a roaring hardwood fire. Once you were a member here, you were beyond the rules.

Then Bruce strode in, his face made florid through biofeedback exercises, his voice much too loud, his words slightly slurred.

"And how the hell have you been?" he said coarsely to the nearest body, clapping it between the shoulders and sending a rare, single-malt Scotch spraying across the equally rare Persian rug.

The victim, a silver-haired executive whose companies rolled steel on five of the seven continents, was a paragon of manners and self-control. His expression was as cold as the interstellar void. "I'm busy, Bruce. Go play your little games elsewhere, if you please."

"Bad day at black rock," Wayne replied, playing his ne'er-do-well role to the hilt. He spied another of his father's business colleagues in deep conversation near the wall of windows. He bulled his way across the room, pausing only to collect a drink from the tight-lipped bartender. With carefully calculated rudeness, he marched between them.

"What a view!" He opened his arms and flung bourbon into one man's face. "There's no place like home—when you're up here and everyone else is down there—"

"Mr. Wayne—?" A butler—not Alfred, of course—appeared at Bruce's side. He laid one hand on Bruce's shoulder and wrapped the other around his wrist. "There's a call for you. If you'll just step this way . . ."

Bruce allowed his arm to be lowered and the pinching hand on his shoulder to guide him toward a darkened doorway. *Mission accomplished.* He had the club's undivided, but discreet, attention. Within hours the old guard would be asking itself the perennial question: What should we do about Tom Wayne's son? A few hours after that, Bruce could count on a call from Harry.

But, as it turned out, he didn't have to wait hours. The door closed behind him, and Bruce was alone in one of the private rooms, face-to-face with a disapproving Harry Mattheson. A shiver of anticipation raced down Bruce Wayne's spine as he divided his consciousness between the actor who would play out the scene and the coldly sober Batman who would be watching Harry with a new eye.

"What is it this time, Bruce—liquor, the wild life, some unholy combination of the two?"

The actor let his jaw hang.

"Look at you. You're a disgrace to your father's name. What's the matter with you? When are you going to take hold and make something of yourself. Something worthwhile?"

The younger man whined alcoholically; the older man scolded. Both seemed completely sincere. Batman looked at the edges for a sign that the disguise was not quite complete, that they were both, in fact actors. The analysis was inconclusive. After all, Harry Mattheson could be the Connection and still care deeply about the ruination of his dead friend's son; the roles were not mutually exclusive. Batman sought the words for a speech that would place Harry's roles in conflict.

"You're not my father!" Bruce shouted. "Stop treating me like the son you never had. You're planning to take your businesses with you to your grave—like all fathers. Like my father did." It was an act, his inner voice said urgently, calming the part of him that would always feel an orphan's anguish. "If I was your son would you teach me what you know? Would you have shown me all your inner secrets, the deals you made to get to the top?"

The actor waited; Batman watched.

Harry opened his mouth and shut it again. He set his glass on a polished wood table and ground his cigar to shreds in a cut-glass ashtray. "Show you? You? Never." He squeezed his lips into pale lines, biting off words Batman dearly wished to hear. Then he stalked out of the room, allowing the door to strike the wall when he beat it open.

For a moment, while he was truly alone, Bruce Wayne shed all his roles and let his tension out with a shuddering sigh. He had as much information as he was likely to get. Mental images of Harry's response, clearer than any photograph or videotape, were printed in his mind's eye. Later, after analysis and reflection, perhaps he'd have an answer.

There was no reason to stay. Harry's stormy exit left him with no need to explain his own. Bruce Wayne left the club scarcely a half hour after he'd entered it.

"Let's go home, Alfred," he said as he settled in the back seat of the limo.

"Did you learn what you wanted to? Is Harry Mattheson the man? Is he the Connection?"

Bruce pulled off the black tie and undid the top studs of

the starched white shirt. He sank back in the upholstery as
Alfred pulled away from the curb. "I don't know. I can't
tell—that says something right there, doesn't it? A man I've
known all my life—and I can't tell what he really is."

"Yes, it does, sir. Yes, it does."

CHAPTER
Eight

CATWOMAN awoke to a rooster crowing before dawn. The sound startled and disoriented her. She lashed out at unfamiliar shadow-shapes, then, as she shed sleep, shook her head with disbelief. She'd seen the henhouse last night and dismissed it as an unsuitable place for sleeping, without giving the inevitable roosters a second thought. For her, roosters had become an urban sound. Cockfighting was another of the East End's ongoing illicit entertainments. Men kept the gaudy, mean-tempered creatures in cages on the fire escapes, turning those vertical sidewalks into noisy obstacle courses. She'd forgotten that a more natural place for a rooster was a henhouse.

Perhaps she had been cooped up in the city too long.

Shaking her head one final time, Catwoman peeled off her costume. Selina's clothes, left overnight in the backpack, were cold and damp. She was shivering by the time she crept out of the toolshed. Many of the convent windows were lit; nuns were notorious early risers, but they had prayer on their mind and weren't likely to look out the curtains as a lone woman marched through the drizzle and climbed over the gate at the end of the driveway.

Selina was wet to the skin and as mean-tempered as any rooster by the time she got to the Riverwyck station. She boarded the first train to Gotham City with a herd of bleary-eyed commuters who ignored her as a stream ignores a boulder sitting in its bed. The train was wonderfully warm. The air thickened with humidity and echoed with snores. Selina kicked off her shoes, drew her op-art knees up under the capacious neon-green sweater, and studied the life cycle of condensation droplets on the steamy windows.

Rose was safe, not sane or sound, but safe. Eddie Lobb wouldn't hurt her again. It seemed to Selina that Rose D'Onofreo should wander out of her thoughts the same way the movement of the train made the droplets migrate to the bottom of the window. But Rose stuck in the middle of Selina's thoughts. She wasn't satisfied knowing that Eddie Lobb couldn't reach her.

"He did it with cats," she murmured to the rhythm of the steel wheels. "He did that to her with cats. That's wrong. Wrong. I'm gonna get him. Eddie Lobb. I'm gonna find him . . ."

The metallic shriek of the brakes in the terminal tunnel roused Selina from an increasingly vengeful and graphic reverie. She joined the throng flowing to the street, only to discover that the drizzle had become a downpour and half of Gotham City was trying to flag a taxi. Shrugging the backpack over her shoulders, she hiked the thirty-odd blocks to home.

A half-dozen cats raised their heads, took a look at the sopping, sullen creature in their midst, and surrendered the bed without a fight.

Selina figured to spend the next few days indoors, sleeping or exercising. Catwoman went out no more than once or twice a week—anything more risked needless exposure to both sides of the law. It was a monotonous life, but Selina liked it that way, considering what it had been before.

Most of the pimps and streetwalkers Selina had known when she first came to Gotham City had vanished; none of the ones who remained had changed for the better. Life on the streets was nasty, brutal, and short. Besides, working with people wasn't the same as being friends with them.

The cats were her friends. Whenever Selina was lonely or bored, she followed their example and curled up for a nap. She was surprised, then, when she didn't fall asleep before she was warm. She thought about Eddie Lobb. She didn't know his face, so she made one up from memory, and slashed it with Catwoman's claws. She made up another face, another punishment. After a while she forgot about sleeping.

There weren't many books around, but one of them was a telephone directory. A half-inch of Lobbs were listed. One was an Edward. Selina checked the address against the directory maps. Her fingers marched to a place north of the East End, near a park. She knew the area. Catwoman prowled there occasionally, when the police were keeping a temporary lid on the drug trade. But she couldn't mentally match buildings with their street addresses.

With more energy than she usually felt the day after Catwoman had prowled—especially a dreary day—Selina headed off to investigate the address she'd memorized. She didn't own an umbrella, just a waterproof military-type sweater and a violently red and orange scarf. There were a hundred ways to remain anonymous in Gotham City, and Selina Kyle knew them all. People might remember the scarf, but they wouldn't remember her.

The building where Rose had lived with Eddie Lobb dominated its corner. A relic of bygone days, when this area was uptown and high class, it had survived decades of neglect to be resurrected as "the Keystone Condominiums—a Matheson investment in Gotham City's future." The doors were thick glass slabs. The lobby beyond abounded with elegance, mirrors and plush sofas with pale upholstery.

No kids, no pets, no unwashed peasants, Selina thought when she was under the awning and headed for the glass doors.

A uniformed doorman scurried to intercept her. She hadn't noticed him sitting on his stool. That was unusual.

"Hey, missy. Who you go see?"

He was a half-head shorter than Selina and easily twenty years older. An amateur would have dismissed him as one more pidgin-speaking alien working a job no American wanted. Except he'd planted himself in the perfect spot to block the doors, and Selina was no amateur. Careful to avoid eye contact, she balanced on the balls of her feet, then shifted her weight ever so slightly toward the doors. The doorman didn't make eye contact, either, but shifted his balance to match hers. He could still stop her, or try to.

There probably weren't more than a handful of doormen in Gotham City who were worth the powder to blow them up, but Eddie Lobb was living in a condo that employed one of them. Rose was safe from everything but her lover while this little gargoyle was guarding the front door. Selina had the advantages of height, reach, and age—not to mention her constant training. She figured that no matter how good he was, she could take him out in under a minute. Of course, a scuffle that lasted thirty seconds drew a crowd; you could make book at one that lasted a full minute. This guy wouldn't be taken in by the scarf. He'd see her face, remember it, and—with her usual luck—he'd agree to go down to the precinct to look at the mug books.

Most of Gotham's finest might not know who Catwoman was, but they had plenty of pictures of Selina Kyle. You couldn't walk the night in stiletto-heeled boots and a cut-out leather dress and not have the cops taking snapshots—right profile, left profile, full front.

"You read, missy?" He stabbed a blunt finger at the brass plate proclaiming: No soliciting. All visitors must be announced. "You got no business here."

"No," Selina agreed. She stepped back, out of critical distance, and the confrontation ended. She spun on her heel, giving him an eyeful of the garish scarf to blur his memory— just in case he was still on duty when she came back.

She would go back. Her mind was churning before the rain struck her face again. Her stomach was churning, too, reminding her that it had been too long since her last meal.

Stuffing her hands in her pants pockets, she fingered the crumpled bills and loose change. More than enough for a meal at the greasy spoon across the street—the one with the window booths and a clear view of Keystone Condominiums from sidewalk to roof.

The cashier scowled when Selina slid into the booth. She scowled right back, and resolved to get herself some new clothes, even if it meant going where she had to look in a mirror before she bought them. The cashier scaled a plastic-sheathed menu onto the table.

"Four-dollar minimum. You still wanna order?"

"A steak—the biggest one you've got—and make it rare, bloody." Selina dug all the money out of her pockets and dribbled it onto the table. The cashier counted eighty dollars and change. "Stop staring and move your butt if you want a tip."

"Yeah, lady. Sure, lady."

Selina turned away and looked out the window. She could hear the cashier muttering as he approached the trench window separating the so-called dining room from the so-called kitchen: "Screw you, bitch . . ."

Sometimes it didn't pay to have extraordinary senses. If she'd been in costume the cashier would have four gashes across his throat. Or, more likely, he wouldn't have opened his mouth in the first place. She pondered the rules of appearances until the food began to arrive and eating was the only thing she cared about. When the last stream of juice had been sopped up by the last morsel of bread, Selina was ready to forgive, forget, and settle into a serious examination of the Keystone.

Its facade was a wedding-cake nightmare. Selina knew next to nothing about architecture, but she knew the building had to be at least a hundred years old. No one today could afford that much god-awful gingerbread masonry, even if they could find the artisans who knew how to make it. The whole place was layers of ledges, and there was a comfortably wide one beneath each rank of windows, probably put there for the convenience of future generations of window washers and cat burglars. There were wrought-iron flower baskets around the windows and widgets that looked like coat hooks sprouting randomly through the walls. Selina didn't know these were the remnants of Victorian scaffolds—and she wouldn't have cared; what she saw was a veritable highway of handholds. With all that helpful metal, there wasn't a window in the Keystone Condominiums that Catwoman couldn't reach.

On the other hand, there could be sixty apartments—more if the developers had chosen profit over style and subdivided. She was going to have to get into the building, learn its guts and sneak a peek at its mailboxes and intercom panel, before Catwoman went to work.

The sour-faced cashier reappeared, cleared the table, and shoved an illegible bill in front of her.

"You can pay me now."

Selina ignored him.

"C'mon, lady. I ain't got all day."

Selina made a show of looking for other customers in the otherwise empty room. "I do," she replied in a dangerously sultry voice. "Gimme a piece of your chocolate pie."

"Didn't you hear me before? There's a four-dollar minimum. I already checked you out. Pie only costs three."

"Then gimme *two* pieces." She smiled. Her even, ivory teeth glistened.

The East End clung to Selina Kyle like a saint's halo and was most easily detected by someone like the cashier who bore it himself. Life was a game in Gotham City. Everyone was always jockeying for a little position.

"And *two* coffees, with cream. Make it separate checks. One after the other."

At the rate she was going through her drug-house cash, Selina figured she'd have to take something from Eddie's apartment. She'd burn that bridge when she got to it. For the moment she had the upper hand with the cashier. His eyes smoldered and she knew he'd clout her if he dared, but he didn't dare. Instead he slunk over to the refrigerator case where tired wedges of chocolate pie were mummified in shrink wrap.

In Gotham's game you didn't lose points for making enemies, so long as you never saw them again. Selina turned her
attention back to the Keystone and ignored the pies when they
arrived.

The gargoyle couldn't perch on that stool twenty-four hours
a day. Selina thought about coming back in the evening.
She discarded the thought. Maybe the management had been
lucky: maybe they didn't know a good doorman from a dead
doornail. Then again, maybe they did, and if they did, and
they'd left him on the day shift, she didn't want to tangle
with the night-shift gorilla.

An oily sheen spread across the surface of the tepid coffee.
The chocolate pie oozed across the crockery plates. The Keystone doorman never missed an opportunity to greet or challenge everyone who approached his domain. He seemed to
know everyone and paused to chat with them. Conversation
didn't dull his vigilance. There'd be no sneaking behind him
while his head was tucked inside an overpriced baby carriage.

Selina had just begun to despair when a young man in a
messenger-service jumpsuit skated around the corner, trailing
a cloud of bright-colored, helium-filled balloons. The sidewalk traffic stopped as he wrangled the balloons under the
Keystone awning and rolled to a stop in front of the doorman.
Their animated conversation was punctuated and obscured by
the bobbing balloons. The messenger removed his skates
reluctantly, but he and the balloons finally got into the lobby.

She held her breath; the gargoyle went back to his stool
without stopping by the intercom. He didn't always live by
the rules. He was human.

Selina knew a place in the East End that did a backroom
business in secondhand uniforms, cash on the counter, no
questions asked. Leaving the greasy spoon, without leaving
a tip, she headed downtown. She was definitely going to have
to lift something from Eddie's apartment, so she stopped by
her apartment and dropped off the garish scarf while picking
up Catwoman's lockpicks. A few hours later, carrying an
excessively large floral arrangement and wearing a shapeless
polyester gabardine jumpsuit that pinched in the crotch, she

reapproached the Keystone awning. She kept the flowers
where they'd obscure her face, and waited for the gargoyle
to scuttle forward.

"Flowers for Miz D'Onofreo."

"Eh? No one here wi' that name."

Selina's heart sank, but she didn't panic. "Not again. They
do this to me every bleeding day." She fumbled with the
bouquet and read the address from the card. The doorman
shook his head and held his ground. Selina played her final
card: "Lobb. Eddie Lobb. You got an Edward Lobb here?
His name's on the receipt, maybe he's got someone staying
with him."

Recognition lit the gargoyle's eyes, but he said nothing.

"Give me a break, okay? I'm on the street, man, if I lose
this job. Just let me take 'em upstairs." Selina did a credible
imitation of despair. "Come on. It's not like I'm going to
bust in and *steal* something, for chrissake."

It was her will against his in the lingering mist and afternoon traffic. An intense young man with designer hair, wire-
rim glasses, and the gray flannel three-piece uniform of the
brokerage trade climbed out of a cab and demanded to know
if his graphite tennis racket had arrived. Another taxi rolled
up and began disgorging luggage. A matron with too much
makeup and a poodle came through the lobby without slowing
down. She expected the doorman to get the door open in
time.

Selina hadn't chosen rush-hour by accident. The doorman
pulled in his will.

"I give you ten minutes. Then I call the cops."

Selina's smile was pure and honest. "Ten minutes. Right.
Apartment five-cee. Ten minutes. Got it." She graciously
opened the door for the poodle matron.

"Seven-gee!" the doorman corrected. "Seven-gee. Mister
Lobb in seven-gee." But he left her holding the door while
he looked for the tennis racket.

Selina would have preferred to take the stairs. She could
always get a better grasp of the guts of a building from the

stairwells than from an elevator, but the doorman was tracking her with his ears. He'd notice if the fire door opened.

Eddie Lobb turned out to live one floor down from the penthouse, at the far end of a well-lit, carpeted corridor. Selina paused. She pretended to have trouble knowing which corridor to take—in case another tenant was spying through his peephole—but she was actually aligning the interior she could now see with the exterior she remembered. After putting a mental check beside a corner cluster of windows, she headed for the door and rang the bell.

She always rang the bell. There was no better way to know if no one was home. She wouldn't mind getting a close look at Eddie Lobb anyway, especially when she said the flowers were for Rose. She rang the bell a second time and studied the array of hardware on the door.

Locks were big business in Gotham City, and, as Catwoman, Selina Kyle had seen them all, from ancient skeleton keys to techno-toy motion detectors and lasers. She'd pegged the Keystone as a two-locks-per-door sort of place, heavy on deadbolts and double cylinders. People who put their faith in cold-forged steel rather than dazzling electronics. A glance up and down the corridor confirmed her overall opinion. Eddie Lobb, with a pair of digital keyless locks and evidence of fiber-optic sensors, was seriously out of step with his neighbors.

Maybe he had more to protect.

Maybe he had more to hide.

Either way, Selina wasn't going to pop those locks in seven minutes. She'd need an hour just to diagnose them, and maybe a day to collect the materials to counteract them—if they could be countered. If they needed to be countered. Doors were supposed to be the easiest way into an apartment— that's why people put locks on them—but they were hardly the only way.

"Who are you?" Selina asked the door. "Fancy locks, frightened woman. What makes you tick, Eddie Lobb?"

She left the flowers propped against the door—let him guess who was sending flowers to his missing girlfriend. With her eyes closed she rechecked her spatial memory. Then, hearing the cables twang and suspecting that the gargoyle was shortchanging her ten minutes, she hurried away from the door.

CHAPTER
Nine

*T*HE evening rush was in full swing when Selina, still dressed in her generic jumpsuit, marched into the lobby of another building from which she expected to get a good look at Eddie Lobb's windows. It was a modern building, with a facade resembling a mirror more than a wedding cake. There were no fire escapes. She announced to the doorman—a more typical specimen of the breed—that she was going to wash some windows. The doorman didn't ask why she was alone, why she wanted to wash windows when it was getting dark, or why she'd wash them when it had just stopped raining. Instead, shrugging, he adjusted the elevator control panel so she wouldn't have to take the stairs to the roof.

On average, even in Gotham City, people were very trusting, very innocent, and very, very stupid.

Selina wrestled the window-washing rig into position and lowered herself over the waist-high wall at the roof's edge. She stopped when she had a clear view of Eddie's apartment. The wrought-iron flower baskets were crusted with pigeon droppings—a sign that he wasn't running electricity through them. If the sun had been shining, she might have had trouble seeing the wires taped to the window glass, but in the waning light, the wire stood out like Interstates on a roadmap.

She unzipped the jumpsuit and dug out a surgical steel chain from around her neck. A small pouch was suspended from it. Removing the walnut-sized lens from the pouch, Selina made a cylinder around it with her fingers and aimed it across the street. In a city well-endowed with gadget-laden characters, Catwoman got by with a set of lockpicks and a bit of polished crystal that could double as a microscope or telescope, depending on her need.

"Breakers," she swore softly. "Damn." Any vertical movement of the window would trip the alarms. Still, the situation could be worse. Selina squinted and focused on the tiny disk in the upper corner of the windowpane to see if it was. She relaxed. The wires had been laid on the glass, not embedded within it. Catwoman could stand on a wedding-cake ledge and remove the central portion of the pane without triggering the alarm—but it wouldn't be her idea of fun.

Eddie Lobb's apartment wrapped unevenly around a corner. She could see most of the windows from her current perch, and although there was no real reason to think that the ones she couldn't see were any less secure than the ones she could, Selina felt obligated—for her alter ego's sake—to check them out. The mirror-sided building didn't offer enough handholds for vertical movement, but with care she could travel horizontally. She climbed out of the rig and traversed the twenty-odd feet she needed for a better view. She hooked a borrowed web-belt into a ventilation louver, turned around, and came close to falling.

The third window from the corner, a window she absolutely believed would get her inside Eddie's apartment, was wide open. Well, not *wide* open, but wide enough that the security system couldn't possibly be working. An utter amateur could waltz right in. Selina plotted Catwoman's route: up the backside of the building to the roof, over the wall, then down to the open window. She curbed her excitement. No good thinking about midnight when the way back to the rig was across a wall of treacherous glass.

She kept a tight rein on her emotions even after she was on the sidewalk, heading home.

It had been a long time—too long a time—since she wanted something as much as she wanted Eddie Lobb. She was invigorated by desire, and not completely certain she liked the feeling.

Selina spent an hour examining the Catwoman costume, from the flexible, shock-absorbing soles of the built-in boots to the razor-claw tips and the tiny slits that allowed her to free her fingertips if she needed to. It was in perfect condition. She dressed and loaded the lockpicks into the concealed thigh pocket—not that she expected to need them—and headed for the Keystone.

The rain had ended; the skies were clear. The East End was quieter than usual, but beyond the slum, people were out for a stroll. Catwoman used roofs and alleys as much as possible, but eventually she had to emerge and dash across a street.

"Lookit, Mommy—a big cat!"

There were strict rules governing this universe. One stated that a human adult didn't notice anything until it happened for the second time. This rule enabled another adult to cross a street in an all-concealing catsuit without being noticed. Unfortunately, the fine print of all the universal rules noted that they were not valid for children. Catwoman couldn't have heard the little boy better if he'd yelled directly into her ear. She turned and nailed the toddler with a killer scowl, then made a run for the nearest alley.

"*Mommy!*"

The child emitted a shriek that aroused everyone on the block. Catwoman dove into a row of battered dumpsters and froze. Her ears were still ringing when the child got his second wind and took the shriek to ultrasonic levels. Despite this, Catwoman heard his parents confer.

"Herb? Herb, did you see that?"

"What, honey?"

"I don't know—a big, black . . . *thing* running—right here, into this alley."

Selina Kyle made herself small. She picked up her feet and braced them on the bottom rail of the dumpster. She closed her eyes and hid the exposed portion of her face. She thought invisible thoughts.

"Timmy's seeing things again. You know how he gets."

The man's voice was clear. The family was at the head of the alley. Selina strained her ears, listening for footfalls. Eventually she heard them fade into the distance. Straightening her spine, Catwoman stared at the sky. It was as dark as it was going to get without a power failure. A haze was moving in; the stars were already gone. But the block was alert. If anyone saw her, it would be for the second time. She stayed where she was, not taking unnecessary chances. Her feet got prickly, then numb. An hour passed, maybe two, or three.

The street sounds changed as the innocent fools retreated to their double-locked homes. Catwoman flexed and stretched, extracting herself from the row of dumpsters, shaking life along her numb nerves. She left the alley and continued on her way without attracting attention. The ascent was easy, and she moved along the ledge without incident. There were curtains on all the windows in Eddie's apartment. Catwoman paused beside each and, hearing nothing, kept going until she reached the open one. It was so criminally inviting that she checked it twice for booby traps. Clinging to the wall, and ready to scoot for the roof, she nudged the window a few inches with her foot. Nothing broke the silence within the apartment, but she waited just the same. There might be a silent alarm downstairs, or a mile away at some security service. She gave them plenty of time to respond before raising the window the rest of the way and lowering herself soundlessly into the room.

She was behind a set of heavy drapes. Again she waited; again there was no need for caution. Parting the drapes, she stepped into the room. She was in a bedroom; there were three doors. One was open and led to a bathroom. The other two were shut. Faint light seeped beneath one but not the other. Deciding that the dark one was probably a closet, Catwoman approached the other. Turning the knob slowly, and lifting up to keep weight off the hinges, she eased it open. She'd guessed right.

Looking down an unlit hallway, she noted another three closed doors before the passage hooked around a corner and—she guessed again—opened into the living room, where the lights had been left on. She listened. She identified and discarded all the street sounds, the murmur of voices—alive and broadcast—coming through the walls. She heard the twang of the elevator cables several walls away, and she heard the plink of a leaky water faucet. This was the loudest and only sound arising within Eddie Lobb's apartment, and it was enough to convince her that she had the place to herself.

Although Selina Kyle survived from month to month by directing Catwoman at the drug gangs in the city's underbelly, her alter ego was in her natural element prowling through undefended homes, sizing up unguarded property. In the beginning, she'd taken what caught her eye, only to discover that personal taste was just about worthless on the black market. Through errors and hard luck, she'd learned that the "good stuff" was generally dull and boring. Monochromes commanded higher prices than rainbows; pieces of charred and twisted metal were worth more than brightly painted figurines. In short, if Selina thought it was ugly, Catwoman knew it was worth taking. The sheer contrariness of art had helped to convince her to stick with taking cash from drug gangs.

Catwoman had figured Eddie Lobb for techno-toys but very little else that would appeal to her personally or professionally. Rounding the corner into the living room, she saw that she was wrong. She and Eddie Lobb were kindred spirits.

Cramped between the ceiling and the sofa, stretching almost the length of the room, a stalking tiger surveyed his domain. The velvet on which he'd been painted, blacker than any Gotham night sky, disappeared behind the shimmering golds and ivories of his well-muscled flanks. His eyes were bronze; his tongue was bloodred. Standing rigid before him, Catwoman heard the faint echo of his roar.

Forget the high-tech locks, the electric tapes on the windows—here was the true guardian of Eddie Lobb's domain. A cliché materialized in Selina's thoughts: How could a man who loved tigers be all bad? Perhaps she had leaped to the wrong conclusions. Perhaps *Rose* was someone who failed to appreciate the majesty inherent in all cats. Perhaps this Eddie Lobb was a man she could get to know, respect, admire . . . and more. She certainly wouldn't steal from him, although her eye swept a number of highly fenceable objects amid an abundance of lesser fare.

Retreating to the hallway, she wondered what Eddie did for a living. More specifically, she wondered if he was a burglar like herself. She could imagine no other way for him to acquire his inventory.

She explored the hallway doors. Two were closets crammed with unlabeled boxes, heavy coats, boots, and other seasonal flotsam. Almost no one in Gotham was rich enough to have an attic or basement. The third door was locked. The mechanism would have yielded to her picks, but as she'd already decided not to take anything, there was no need to use them. The fourth door took her back where she'd started.

Leaving the door open for the light, Catwoman studied the room. It was Rose's room. She recognized the scent, but Eddie's presence was equally strong. There was another velvet painting crowding the bed—a bare-breasted woman astride a tiger. Catwoman found this painting less appealing than the one in the living room. The chairs were dark and heavy, with plush upholstery and claw feet. The bed was an antique with sturdy posts rising from the corners. The overall style might best be described as early bordello—the sort of thing men thought was feminine.

Belatedly Catwoman realized the light was wrong; she looked up and saw a mirror over the bed. She began to have reservations about Eddie Lobb. Her curiosity grew; her reluctance to probe his secrets waned. She looked in the closet; nothing extraordinary, nothing masculine, either. There was a tall dressing cabinet with carved wooden doors and a woefully inadequate lock. After lifting the firm tips and sliding her fingers through the slits, she went to work with her picks. The doors swung open. Her costume obscured her reflection in the vanity mirror, except for the scowl on the unmasked portion of her face and the flash of steel as she replaced the pick in its pocket. Like any self-respecting cat, she had no love for her own image and quickly looked elsewhere.

She looked down at a fancy tray covered with perfume bottles and, behind the bottles, closer to the mirror, at two small globes that hovered in the shadow and glowed with their own light. Driven by curiosity, Catwoman reached toward them. Her fingers stopped short and began to tremble.

The globes were eyes—artificial eyes glued into the preserved head of a half-grown Siberian tiger.

Selina knew it was a Siberian tiger thanks to the Wilderness Warriors, whose quarterly newsletter was the only piece of mail she looked forward to and read over and over until she'd committed it to memory. She learned things about the great cats she'd never imagined as a little girl, but mostly she learned that her favorite predators were doomed. Their habitats were vanishing. They could not distinguish between prey that belonged to no one and prey that belonged to a local farmer or herdsman. But, worst of all, they were ravaged by poachers—greedy treasure-hunters to whom the words *endangered species* meant *higher profit*.

She knew that Eddie Lobb could not have acquired the head—which she slowly realized was the lid of a box—in an honest way. Traffic in endangered animals—alive, stuffed, or in pieces—was illegal. It wasn't the illegality that got to Catwoman, though. It was the immorality. Eddie Lobb loved tigers, but he didn't love them freely. Unsatisfied with pictures or statues, he craved the tiger itself. He didn't seem to mind that the tiger had to die first, and that made him as sin-heavy as the poacher who laid the trap and pulled the trigger.

Selina understood the temptation. She had to touch the head a second time. She shuddered when the stiff, coarse fur brushed her exposed fingertips. The head was bigger than her nameless gray kitten, but otherwise the faces were the same. No wonder Rose had freaked out in the mission kitchen.

Suddenly light-headed and weak-kneed, Catwoman sank to her knees, still holding the relic at arm's length.

How could a man who loved tigers be all bad?

This was how.

THIS was how.

The urge to leave grew strong but was dwarfed by the roar of curiosity. Shoving the box back into the cabinet, slamming the doors without regard for who might hear the sound, Catwoman raced down the hall, to the locked door. Her picks were useless in her trembling hands. She resorted to force, slamming her shoulder against the door until it sprang open. The room was dark, too dark for her sensitive eyes. She groped for a toggle switch, found it, and flipped it up.

A gasp escaped her lips. Her stomach collapsed and did a back roll. There was another cliché in her thoughts:

Curiosity killed the cat.

The room was obscene, an abomination. There were no other words to describe it. Stitched-together tiger hides covered the walls. A complete pelt, with head, feet, and tail attached, sprawled across the floor. Mounted heads were everywhere, some stuffed and lifelike, others rendered down to glistening bone. A table stood on tiger legs. The chair behind it had tiger ribs for its back and cheetah skulls for finials. There was more—at least a hundred objects made from tiger hide, teeth, or bone—but Catwoman had already seen too much. Nauseous, unable to breathe or think, she staggered out of the room, shutting the door behind her. Tears oozed from her eyes. The black mask captured them and held them against her cheeks where they burned like acid.

Catwoman never cried. The alien sensation unnerved her and threatened her spirit. She slid down to her knees and wrapped her arms protectively around her head. She prayed for rage and hatred to sustain her. The fire rose slowly, restoring her strength, drying her tears. She slipped the caps over her fingertips and bared her teeth at the closed door.

She couldn't reenter the room. The fire wasn't burning hot enough, not yet, so she attacked the door and the frame around it, leaving deep scratches in the wood.

"You'll die, Eddie Lobb." Catwoman's hoarse whisper filled the empty apartment. "You'll die for this. You'll meet the spirit of every tiger, every cat, who died to satisfy your greed and lust. You'll beg for mercy. But it won't come, and death will be only the beginning of your punishment."

CHAPTER
Ten

CATWOMAN made her way back to her apartment. She headed directly to the training mats, without pausing to shed the costume. Ever cautious of their benefactor's moods, the four-footed cats made themselves scarce. With glowing, green-gold eyes they watched from safe places as the two-footed cat contorted herself.

Selina intended to work out until she collapsed. Her superb condition fought against her. Her body routinely made the near-magical switch from ordinary physical metabolism to sheer will and determination. Through the dead hours when the city was almost quiet, Selina pursued exhaustion without catching it.

With her palms on the floor, her back arched, and her toes pointed toward heaven, she straightened her arms into a handstand, then flexed them until her skull bumped the floor. She repeated this act—the impoverished gymnast's bench press—ten . . . twenty . . . fifty times before swinging her body down for an equally tortured version of a sit-up. In time, lactic acid and dehydration made every move an exercise in pain, but Selina's mind remained sharp. The images she'd brought out of Eddie Lobb's apartment grew more vivid and real, more horrifying with each repetition.

Her vision blurred as sweat trickled across her face. She let her eyes close, then opened them with a shudder. She lost her balance. She tucked and rolled into a cross-legged sitting position with her back curled. With a defeated sigh, Selina relaxed. Her forehead rested against her ankles. Her eyes were open, staring at nothing. Her mind's eye was filled with tigers, lions, cheetahs, panthers, and leopard; skulls and bones; and glowing, reproachful eyes.

What are you going to do about us? they asked in overlapping chorus.

Selina made a fist and pounded weakly on the floor beside her.

"I'll kill him. I swear I'll kill him."

What are you going to do about us?

She knew how to kill Eddie Lobb: stake out his home. His kind—the kind that collected relics and hid them behind layers of locks—always came back to restore itself amid forbidden treasure. All she had to do was watch and wait. She could feel her claws sink into his neck; feel the flesh separate as she pulled upward, outward; see the look in his eyes, just before he died, when he realized that a cat had come to claim him.

Then what? Did she leave Eddie Lobb in his blood, surrounded by his obscene collection, for the Gotham City Police to find? Did killing Eddie Lobb end anything but Eddie Lobb? What about Rose, what about the collection?

One of those questions was pathetically easy to answer. With regard to Rose D'Onofreo, Selina Kyle couldn't have cared less. Rose was an accident, an innocent, insignificant and no longer important. If the nuns could salvage her mind, so much the better; if not, well, that was okay too. What Eddie Lobb had done to Rose was a consequence of his corruption. If it hadn't been Rose, it would have been someone else—it would become someone else if Selina and Catwoman didn't stop Eddie Lobb.

But what about his relics, his fetishes? Did she try to

remove them herself? In garbage bags tossed into an alley or dumpster? Should she turn his apartment into a funeral pyre? That would put his neighbors at risk. Were they more or less innocent than Rose?

Selina shook her head violently and growled with primitive anguish.

"I don't know what to do," she confessed, regretting—for a moment—that she lived without friends or family, with only the cats and Catwoman as advisers. For another moment she considered going to the mission. Her thoughts reeled—rather like seeing every scene from a movie simultaneously. She watched herself enter Old MoJo's office, tell her tale, while the veiled woman laughed herself into a frenzy. The humiliation Selina felt was real, even if the scenes she imagined were not.

She sat where she was, not moving but not falling asleep, either—simply waiting for things to change, to get worse.

Worse came in the form of small piece of warm, wet sandpaper rasping her cheek: a cat harvesting the salt of her exertions. Selina cocked her head and squinted. The gray tiger kitten. Had she expected anyone else? Pretty soon she was going to have to give the little guy a name. Slipping her hand beneath his plump barrel-belly, Selina hoisted him into the air. She swiveled her wrist, thinking about names. He gouged the air with half-grown claws and bared his milk teeth.

"Not afraid of anything, are you?"

Selina lowered him to the floor. He arched his back once his toes touched down. His tail shot up and the soft kitten-fur fluffed like milkweed down. He hissed mightily. She reached for him; he stood his ground, undaunted by her larger claws.

"So what if I'm a hundred times bigger than you, right? You're a regular warrior—" Her thoughts nose-dived inward. Selina forgot the kitten attacking her fingers. "A regular warrior. A Wilderness Warrior."

The tension and anguish evaporated. Selina had the solution. She'd had it from the beginning without recognizing it. The militant defenders of predators, the ones who had taught her how to recognize the problem, would surely have the wherewithal to solve it. The Wilderness Warriors would deal with Eddie Lobb's collection while Catwoman dealt with Eddie himself. Possibilities, probabilities, and—she hoped—inevitabilities clamored for her attention.

"Later."

Now that she had an answer, Selina could feel the abuse she'd heaped on her body, and smell the rank costume. She kept it on while she stood in the shower, scrubbing it, then herself, in the steamy water. She quenched her thirst in a final cold rinse. After stamping on the catsuit and wringing it out with her hands, Selina threw it over the shower head and, wrapped in a towel, left the bathroom.

The sun was up. The room was painfully bright and the cats were demanding breakfast. Selina couldn't remember the taste of her greasy-spoon steak, but the effort of opening a can of tuna fish seemed too much to contemplate. She filled a bowl with dry cat food and put it on the floor for the cats to fight over, then dug a handful out for herself. The kibble crunched like pretzels and tasted much better than she expected. After chomping through a second handful, she left the bag propped against the bed.

The room was bright, summertime hot, and stuffy when Selina woke up in the middle of the afternoon. Her head was throbbing; no wonder the cats preferred canned food. Fending off the light with an upraised hand, she navigated to the refrigerator. There was a double-sized container of orange juice in the freezer. She was too impatient to let it thaw properly and ate it like ice cream instead. The effect was indescribable and nearly instantaneous. When her eyes came back into focus, Selina was ready to take on the world.

Despite writing the Wilderness Warriors address on an envelope every month or so, Selina had not wasted much thought on their organization or location. She sent them money anonymously and they did Good Things with it. She didn't feel the need to check up on them, and they had no idea who she was. It had seemed, to Selina, a perfect relationship.

She was somewhat disappointed, then, to find herself on a Gotham side street in a neighborhood that was just a bit cleaner, a bit safer, a bit luckier than the East End. The street was lined with six-story brownstone buildings that looked fundamentally no different than her own—except that the walls weren't covered with profane graffiti, no one was passed out on the steps to the front doors, and every building had a phalanx of garbage cans securely chained to those steps. Trees grew behind stout metal fences at intervals along the sidewalk; someone had taken the trouble to plant daffodils in the soil around them.

These were the differences between poverty and comfort in Gotham City.

The Warriors' banner—black with a central white circle containing the crimson silhouette of a watchful lion—hung from a pole that grew out of a basement-level window. Selina made her way around the ranks of garbage cans to the locked and grated door hidden beneath the steps. A little plastic plaque requested her to look up at the camera after ringing the bell, but aside from the banner there was nothing to tell Selina that this was the button she wanted to push. She was braced for an argument or an apology when the inner door swung open.

"Hi—come on in. Don't you just hate those things?" A woman in her twenties with freckles, green eyes, and reddish-brown hair pointed at the camera. "They make everyone feel like a criminal." She stood in harm's way, holding both inner and outer door open. Selina guessed she hadn't been in Gotham more than a month.

"I disconnected the silly thing when I started working, but they"—she tilted her head toward a Pullman corridor of closed doors leading away from the door—"say it's for my own good. I'm not in Indiana anymore. I told them: In Indiana we know that locks only keep the honest people out. If I can't trust the people who come to Wilderness Warriors, then who can I trust in Gotham City? And they said no one."

Selina wedged into the corridor and got the doors shut behind her. The other woman barely paused for breath as she led the way into the front office.

"What can the Wilderness Warriors do for you today? I'm here all by my lonesome, so I hope it's not too complicated. Are you a member? Would you like to join? I've got copies of our newsletter here—" She reached toward one of several precarious piles on her desk and noticed the videotape sitting atop it. "Would you like to see some amazing footage of eagles? There's this woman in Alaska who films eagles flocking to fish the salmon run. Eagles, flocking! This is just video; it's not as sharp as film would be. She's asking us for money to film it next year. She's going to need a ton of equipment to do it right, and a ton of money. We'll probably say no. But this is pretty impressive. There's a VCR set up in back. I could play it for you. If you want—?"

"No," Selina said, seizing the opportunity to get a word in. "I'm not interested in birds. I know of a man, right here in Gotham City. I want to report him. His apartment looks like the Great White Hunter gone berserk. It's all real; none of it's legal. Tigers mostly, Bengal, Sumatran, and Siberian. I want the Warriors to go in there and clean him out."

The girl didn't hesitate before saying: "Real tigers . . . ? Here, in the city? I don't know, shouldn't you call the police, or the zoo?"

Selina leaned out over the desk, then exploded with descriptions of the relics that she had seen in Eddie Lobb's apartment. By the time she was finished, the young woman behind the desk was speechless. Satisfied that she'd gotten the message and the images across, Selina took a step backward and waited. After a few moments the young woman began fussing uselessly with papers on her desk. Selina's heart sank.

Bonnie—the girl said her name was Bonnie—was sincerely upset, that much was obvious, but, she explained, she was new in the office, in the city. She was here on an internship; the ink on her college diploma was scarcely dry. She thought they'd need proof, pictures at least, sworn statements, and even then, Bonnie wasn't sure what the Wilderness Warriors could do. They'd never targeted an individual. There might be legal complications. The other Warriors—all five of them—were in Washington for the week.

"We're really a lobbying organization, not as activist as I thought we were. But we're going to sign a statement on the Southeast Asian rain forest and the impact of deforestation with a whole bunch of other groups. That's why everybody's gone. Big photo opportunity. But that's no help to you, is it?"

"No," Selina replied, more civilly than she'd expected. She was deeply disappointed. She'd given these people thousands of dollars, and they were worthless when she needed them. Her natural inclination was to take negative feelings out on the nearest target. Heaven knew, Bonnie should have been an ideal target. Her clothes weren't fancy—they even looked comfortable—but they matched, they even matched the eye shadow she was wearing. Bonnie looked like she'd stepped out of a catalog. Bonnie looked like everything Selina Kyle wasn't. She should have been the ideal target. Besides, she never shut up.

But Selina's heart wasn't in it.

"Look, I'm sorry," Selina heard herself saying. "I should've called first. I should've found out more about what you do. I'm sorry for wasting your time."

Three quick steps and Selina was back on the street, back at square one with Eddie Lobb's relics staring into her mind's eye. The Wilderness Warriors had seen the last of her money, but there was no satisfaction in the thought.

"Wait! Hey! Wait—don't go away! I've got an idea."

Bonnie's voice and the sound of running. Selina squared her shoulders and kept going. She didn't need ideas from the phony warriors. She heard the footfalls getting closer, but it never occurred to her that someone, a complete stranger, would presume to lay a hand on her.

"Hey! Stop a minute and listen."

Selina had no choice. It took every mote of energy within her to keep from killing the woman; there was nothing left for benign movement or conversation.

"I've got an idea. If you can get me into this guy's apartment, *I'll* take pictures. When everybody gets back, I'll just keep on them until they give and decide to do something. I'll plaster the walls with enlargements; they won't be able to turn around without seeing stuffed tigers looking back at them. We're supposed to be the Wilderness Warriors. If this is as bad as you say it is, we've *got* to do something. You and me. You get me in, I'll take photos. I've got *all* the equipment. Stills, tape, even film-film if we need a pan shot to get the whole effect."

Selina's heart was beating again, and she was breathing. Her voice was still somewhere in the next state. But with Bonnie close by, no one else needed a voice.

"Omygod." Bonnie clapped her hands over her mouth. The skin surrounding her freckles flared blush-red. "The *door*. Omygod—I'm locked out!" She staggered back a step, colliding with a row of garbage cans. The blush died suddenly; her face was almost gray. "My keys. Everything. I'm locked out of the office, of my apartment. I don't have any money— Omygod. Omygod. What am I going to do?"

It went against everything Selina had believed since she arrived in Gotham City, and everything that had brought her here, but she reached out and put her arm around Bonnie's shaking shoulders. "Maybe you're not really locked out. Let me give it a try. I have a way with locks sometimes."

A few minutes later the two women were in the Wilderness Warriors office again.

"Wow—I don't believe you did that. You just shook the door a couple times and it opened. Wow," Bonnie repeated for about the tenth time.

"It wasn't anything." It hadn't been quite that easy, but she was certain Bonnie hadn't seen her palm the steel pick. Selina certainly wasn't going to reveal her secrets.

"Oh, it was. I thought I was in real trouble. Now you've

got to let me help you with the guy with the tigers. Fair is fair. When can you get me inside?''

Layers upon layers of doubt showed on Selina's face—so many that Bonnie herself noticed.

"I'm not afraid and I'm a good photographer." She spotted the wall clock: a few minutes after five. "I could show you. I brought all my gear from college. I really thought this internship was going to be more than answering telephone calls. I thought they were going to send me someplace . . ."

Selina shook her head, retreating for the door as she did.

"Please. Please give me a chance . . . ? What's your name, anyway? If we're going to work together to get this guy, I've at least got to know your name."

The doorknob pressed against Selina's palm, but she didn't turn it. "Selina. Selina Kyle."

"Selina. I like that. Moon goddess. Diana. The Huntress. What a great name for a Wilderness Warrior. Who ever heard of a Wilderness Warrior—or any kind of warrior—named *Bonnie*? Look, it's after five. I can lock up, leave *with* my keys, and we can do dinner—I've always wanted to say that: 'do dinner'—and we can make our plans. I'm great at making plans, too. . . ."

None of Selina's formidable defenses was designed to protect her from friendship. She was completely tongue-tied, which someone else might have noticed, but not Bonnie. She took silence for consent and quickly shut down the office.

"Where do you want to go for dinner? I don't know very many places. I've only been in Gotham a few weeks. I know a nice little Italian restaurant, but it gets crowded. Is that a problem? People might overhear us talking. Do you think we should worry about people listening—I mean, if we're going to be breaking into someone's place? Maybe we should do take-out instead. Or I could cook—"

"Wait." Selina found her voice. "Who said anything about breaking into anything?"

"Well, you picked the lock, didn't you? I mean, I'm not from Kansas. I already tried wiggling it, and it didn't open for me. I know you didn't just wiggle it, but I didn't see what you did do. So you must be good. And how else would you know about this guy we're going after, right? He's not a friend of yours, or even the friend of a friend, right? So— should we go to the restaurant or do take-out? What do you think?''

"Take-out," Selina said meekly, and followed the still-chattering woman out the door.

CHAPTER
Eleven

*B*RUCE Wayne sat in his family mansion's library surrounded by open books in several languages, none of them less than forty years old. There was also a stack of newspapers, many proclaiming a new world order that looked remarkably like the older one, and the Gotham City telephone directory.

According to the Bible, mankind spoke a common language until the descendants of Noah assaulted the ramparts of heaven with the Tower of Babel. The visitors were not welcome. The tower was smashed, and the next morning the survivors had lost the ability to understand each other. Although premeditated murder had appeared much earlier in the book, warfare, strife, and intolerance grew in the ruins of Babel. If the story were taken literally, then the Tower of Babel was a ruined ziggurat in Babylon, now known as Iraq, where warfare, strife, and intolerance were still going strong. If, on the other hand, the story was a metaphor, then the Tower could have been built in many different places, including Bessarabia.

"It's as if all the leaders of the world, all the scholars, politicians, and educators, got together in 1919 and said: The world's too complicated this way. Let's make it simple. We'll pretend these places and these people didn't exist. We'll redraw the maps, change the way everything is spelled, and in fifty years no one will be the wiser.''

Alfred acknowledged Bruce's complaint with a disdainful sniff as he adjusted the draperies to let in the early-morning light. Never one to do things by halves, his friend and employer had returned from that inauspicious meeting with Harry Mattheson, gotten a few hours' sleep, and then plunged recklessly into old-fashioned research. Once again Batman had pushed himself to the limit.

"It almost worked," the butler said when golden light flowed into the room. "We had superpowers, and you'll have to admit, everything was very simple when you were growing up. When computers came along, no one paid any attention to the old hatreds and conflicts.''

Bruce slapped a book shut. A plume of dust billowed through the streaming light. "But wrong. Here in the United States, we only have five hundred years of history—by the rest of the world's standards, that's not enough time to build a decent grudge. The farther back I go, the more hatred I find, and it never goes away. Those men in 1919 didn't simplify anything; they only added another layer of oppression. There are at least three groups of people who could be Gordon's Bessarabians, and whichever one it is, they're probably planning to use their weapons on the other two.''

Alfred frowned, more at the dust clinging to the books than at Bruce's commentary. "When I was growing up, the big fear was anarchy. *Balkanization*, my teachers called it. Communism and fascism looked like acceptable solutions to the problem. Big powers to keep the little ones in check. I believe I recall that Bessarabia is in the general area of the Balkans.''

"That's it.'' Bruce rose from his chair. He flexed and stretched his shoulders until the ligaments snapped, then loudly closed all the books.

"What is, sir?''

"All we see is names in books and on maps. We hear about people fighting and killing each other because they want to spell their names with Latin letters rather than Cyrillic. They see independence as the freedom to speak and write the language of their parents. We see it in terms of money. And so we call them foolish, ignorant, and backward. We can't see what they see—or maybe we just don't want to.''

"I know I don't want to, sir," Alfred confessed. "It seems so sad, so wasteful. Fighting like that over things that aren't important."

Bruce opened a window and cleansed his lungs with a yawn. "That's only because no one ever told you that you couldn't speak English, or call yourself Alfred."

He took a step back from the window. Alfred hurried forward to close it.

"I'm going to Gotham. I think I know where I can find one of my three potential terrorist Bessarabians. I'm going to listen to them until I understand why they're ready to go to war with their neighbors. No need to make dinner."

Alfred straightened the drapes stiffly. They didn't argue, not after all the years and all the secrets. They knew what could be changed and what could not. And when there was nothing left to say, they said nothing.

"Will you need one of the cars, sir?" Alfred's voice was carefully expressionless.

"No." Which meant that Batman was going, not Bruce Wayne.

"Very well, sir." Alfred paused by the door. "Good hunting, sir."

The Batmobile always drew stares as it cruised down the highway, but here in one of Gotham's peripheral, ethnic neighborhoods—where Batman did not have a prepared safe house—it drew a crowd. The vehicle was impervious to theft or vandalism; the children who reached out to touch it did not leave so much as a fingerprint on its black matte surface. They retreated when the fully costumed Batman got out, but he had no sooner sealed the doors and set the alarms than he felt a tentative tug on the cap.

"Batman," the dark-eyed moppet said, spreading his arms as he released the cloth. *"Drakul."*

Batman was more accustomed to being surrounded by armed criminals than grinning children. He smiled awkwardly and looked for a path to the sidewalk. The other children chattered rapidly, then joined the boldest one in holding their arms outstretched. They all jumped up and down, flapping their arms, raising their voices, and drawing the attention of their elders. Feeling a little trapped, Batman imitated their posture, allowing the cape to billow from his arms and shoulders. They shrieked with delighted terror and ran away.

The day's business was not getting off to a good start. Within the costume, Bruce Wayne wished he was without it as well. He was a world away from the docks and slums of central Gotham. His confidence that he could learn anything from these wary immigrants looked like another example of American arrogance.

He heard a woman scream. Trouble sounded like trouble in every language. Without hesitation, he bolted down the sidewalk. The sound had come from a small bakery. Batman took in the whole shop with a single glance as he came through the door. A stocky woman with a bright kerchief knotted over her hair stood behind the open cash register. Her eyes widened when she beheld the dark apparition looming in her doorway. She staggered backward until the racks of fresh black bread supported her. Clutching the front of her blouse, she tried and failed to scream.

Batman saw the kitchen through the bread racks. He saw the open, swinging back door as well.

"I'll be back with your money."

She nodded as he went by, but did not seem at all reassured.

The kitchen emptied into a tenement courtyard fundamentally similar to every other courtyard jumble of concrete and weeds in the city. Relying on instinct and experience, Batman eyed the scene. There were two likely ways out: a tunnel-like alley between two buildings on the far side, and a fire-escape ladder someone had left in the lowered position. There were open windows behind the fire escape; a few were hung with curtains that fluttered slowly. Since there was no breeze, Batman reached the obvious conclusion.

Batman climbed quickly, but cautiously, making as little noise as possible, especially after he heard voices on the roof above him. Now he was grateful for the costume and the options it provided. Removing a fist-sized object from his belt, he aimed it at the wall just below the roofline but several yards beyond the fire escape. He thumbed a lever, and a filament hissed out of his hand. It hit the wall with no more sound than a pebble might make. A finger of smoke extended out from the wall as the adhesive coating of the plug bonded with the brick. Batman tested the line, then leaped away from the fire escape.

The filament shortened as he swung. He braced himself for the impact, reaching up for the cement slabs at the top of the wall with his free hand. With a practiced effort, he conserved momentum as he vaulted over the cornice, releasing the filament at the last moment. He landed in an alert crouch.

Time froze.

Three men looked up from a pillowcase they held open between them. They gaped with astonishment. They smiled. The fourth man on the roof, the Batman, decided the order of attack. He folded the fingers of his right hand into a flat-knuckled fist. He'd take the first two with the energy he stored in the bunching muscles of that arm. He'd take the third, the burliest of the men and also the one on the far side of the pillowcase, with a left forearm across the windpipe.

Surging forward with a shout, Batman dropped the first with a hammer punch to the solar plexus; the man never saw what hit him. He took the second with a roundhouse blow to the chin; the victim had time to see, but no time to react. The third dropped to his knees and held out his empty hands; he spoke the same strange language as the children in the streets. Batman ignored him and reached down for the pillowcase. It was heavier than he expected. He glanced in and saw why:

They'd taken the money from the bakery—about forty

dollars in small bills and change—but the object of the robbery had been the small, dark painting in a golden frame.

The first thief was beginning to move and make noise. The second remained out cold. Batman indicated that the kneeling man and the groaning man should carry their companion down the fire escape. In the distance he could hear a police siren. He hoped it was coming here. He hoped the officers would be willing and able to ask a few questions on his behalf.

The siren grew louder, then was silent. Two officers met Batman and the alleged perpetrators in the now-crowded bakery. The terrified woman ran upstairs. While the older cop went after her, the younger tried to oblige the near-legendary caped crusader. He fired off a barrage of unfamiliar sounds that were similar to the language Batman had heard on the street and roof. But, apparently, not similar enough. Batman suspected the sullen thieves knew exactly what had been said, but they shook their heads and gestured in confusion.

"Can't keep up with them, sir," the fair-skinned young man said, automatically assuming that Batman outranked him in law-enforcement matters. "Used to be just Russians and Poles and they could somehow talk to each other. Now it's everything: Russians, Poles, Bulgarians, Ukrainians—you name it—and they won't talk to each other."

"He understood you, I think."

"I'm sure he did, sir. I wouldn't bet against him understanding everything we're saying. Moscow made 'em learn two languages—Russian and English. We'll take them down to the station and they'll talk. We've got a room down there now that looks straight out of the KGB headquarters. We sit 'em in there for a couple of hours, and they're ready to talk. Old habits die hard, I guess."

The older cop came downstairs shaking his head. "We can take 'em down and book 'em, but what's the use? She won't talk to us. She won't even say the money was stolen from her, or that saint picture. She doesn't want anything to do with the police." The pillowcase, the money, and the picture were spread across the counter near the cash register. He began bundling them together.

The younger cop restrained his partner. "That icon's probably been in her family a long time. They had to hide it all those years; they could've been imprisoned or sent to Siberia just for having it. And after all that, they bring it here. I know it's physical evidence, Cliff, but if she's not going to press charges anyway . . . ?"

Cliff rubbed his thumb across the flaking gilt, weighing the charges. "What's this stuff worth, anyway?"

"A lot more to her than to us," the young officer said firmly.

Swearing softly to himself, Cliff put the icon back on the counter. Another car had arrived: backup transportation to the station. "Okay, let's get outta here." He turned to Batman. "You coming too?"

"Do you need me?"

"Nope." The single word contained all the ambivalence the uniformed police felt toward costumed free-lancers.

"Then I'll stay here. Maybe I can convince the woman to go to the station."

"Yeah. Sure. A guy in a cape, a mask, and circus clothes. Maybe she'll think it's Halloween."

Batman stood without comment as the policemen and their prisoners left. He was still standing, hoping the woman would come downstairs, when another young man came down instead. He looked to be in his early twenties, and he didn't look at all surprised to see Batman. He *was* surprised to see the icon. Very surprised. Very relieved. And very quick to hide what he had revealed.

"My mother would thank you, but America frightens her," he said in accented but confident English. "America is not what any one of us expected. But home has changed so much, too. Where else can we go?" He glanced around the room, obviously looking for something else. He found it—a velvet-covered box carelessly thrown against the wall. Batman had not noticed it before, nor had the police. The youth retrieved the box and carefully fit the icon into it. He held the closed box tightly against his chest.

Things weren't adding up. Batman's curiosity acquired a

razor edge. "You're Russian?" he asked with exaggerated doubt. "From the Soviet Union . . . Russia?"

"This week, the Commonwealth of Independent States; yes. Last week, the Union of Soviet Socialist Republics. Russian, yes, but *Russia*, no."

Forearmed as Batman was with his library researches, this made sense. "You come from one of the other republics, then. One of the new Baltic countries? Latvia, Lithuania, Estonia . . ." If the youth had been here any length of time, he knew how Americans loved to show off their limited knowledge of events on the far side of the world. But Batman hadn't chosen this particular block at random, and when the youth shook his head with a condescending smile, Batman knew he'd chosen correctly.

"Moldavian Soviet Socialist Republic," the youth said.

"Last week. This week the Moldovan Sovereign Republic." Batman hoped he'd managed to convey the new spelling of the name.

He had. The youth muttered words not included in any orthodox Russian dictionary, then spat emphatically at the floor. "Stalinist pigs."

Stalin was, after all, Georgian, not Russian, and pigs seemed to be universally reviled.

"And the men who tried to steal the icon?"

"Moldavian pigs," the youth announced, using Russian orthography. "My family did not ask to live in their filthy little country, but we came, we built the factories, and we worked in them. It is ours now, and they would take it from us . . . for *Rumania*. Stinking Rumanian gypsies."

The mask helped Batman keep his thoughts to himself. Perhaps Alfred had a point about Balkanization. "The police here don't take kindly to immigrants importing their wars with them . . . or exporting weapons back home, either."

"We send money back, yes. And food. Much food." The youth's expression had grown wary. "But weapons, no. Already too much guns." He eased a step closer to the stairs.

"Tell me about the icon. To whom does it really belong? Not you, and not the woman upstairs who isn't your mother."

The youth's knuckles whitened as he clutched the box tighter. "It is ours. The family that owned it are all dead. That is true. But they were *Russian*. It is ours, to do with what we want. To give. To sell. Not theirs. We have rights. Americans understand rights."

The youth was one of millions of ethnic Russians forcibly dispersed through the former Soviet Empire—in his case, the parcel of land Western textbooks called Bessarabia. The Moldavians, or Moldovans, wished to erase the artificial border between their land and Rumania. They had a point: The difference between the Moldovan language and the Rumanian language was less than the difference between American English and English English. Except the Moldovans had been compelled, since 1940, to write it with the alphabet known variously as Soviet, Russian, Cyrillic, or Greek, while the Rumanians used Latin letters, just like English.

Bruce Wayne had, however, found three potential terrorist factions beneath the Bessarabian label.

"What about the Gagauzi?" Batman asked. "What rights do the Gagauzi have?"

Crestfallen, the youth relaxed his grip on the box. His knuckles turned red as the blood flowed back to them. So did his face. He hadn't believed in Batman, not really, not the way the swine Moldavians did—thinking he was an incarnation of their national hero, Vlad Drakul. But Batman knew about the Gagauzi. How many Americans knew about the Gagauzi? There were only about a hundred and fifty thousand of them.

"It is"—the youth groped for the word—"like buying and selling, but without money. The Gagauzi have sheep, they have vineyards, they have tobacco. The sheep are . . . not so good. The wine, the tobacco, these are better than money. The Moldos will try to crush the Gagauzi first. Already they say: learn our language, do things our way. The Gagauzi see writing on the wall, yes? They do not like us Russians very much: Moscow said, learn our language, do things our way. But in the beginning, we had the army, and the army came from Moscow to protect them. Now Moscow is . . .'' He mimed blowing out a candle. "No army. Just us and the Gagauzi. The Gagauzi and us.

"American patriot, Benjamin Franklin, says: We hang together, or for sure we hang apart.''

The sheepherders Tiger mentioned on the dock. It all fit together. There were moments when Batman regretted the mask because there were moments when he wanted to bury his head in his hands. Instead he said: "So the Gagauzi give you—the Russians in Moldavia—wine and tobacco that you barter with other Russians—in Russia itself—for . . . icons. . . ? And you sell the icons here, in America, to get money to buy guns for the Gagauzi to fight the Moldovans?''

The youth shook his head. "No money. We give the icons to the scar-faced man. Two already, this is third and last. After that. Nothing. Not for us. Finished. What the Gagauzi do, we don't see, we don't know. Very simple.''

A bell rang inside Batman's head—*the scar-faced man?* There were undoubtedly thousands of scar-faced men in Gotham City. But lightning did strike in the same place, many times. And Batman's heart warmed with the knowledge that he knew where to find the right scar-faced man. He curbed his enthusiasm. There was still more to be learned here.

"And the icon you're holding? The one the Moldovans would have stolen successfully, if I had not intervened?''

The youth's face was as rigid as Batman's mask.

"They know it's still here. You know that they'll be back for it.''

The youth began shaking. "So far, what you call down payment. This—this is payment: the best, the most valuable. Somehow, the swine find out. Without I bring the icon, no payment, no exchange. The Gagauzi, they will blame us. Then it is everyone against everyone else.''

Alfred definitely had a point.

Batman needed only a few minutes to persuade the youth to tell him when and where the payment was to be made and to entrust him with the icon until that time.

"They will try to steal it from you," the youth said when the box was out of his hands. "They will stop at nothing. They will hire your enemies and send them after you."

Another light burned in Batman's head. "I'll count on it," he said as he left.

CHAPTER
Twelve

C ATWOMAN stood with her back against the bathroom
wall, contorting herself while keeping one eye on the
medicine-cabinet door where the apartment's only
mirror was hung. The inspection was not a normal part of her
routine, but neither was keeping appointments or bringing a
companion along on a prowl, both of which were going to
happen in the next few hours. With a final tug on the mask
to cover her eyebrows, the black-costumed woman decided
that enough was good enough and reached for the pull chain
attached to the light.

"I don't believe you're doing this," she told her reflection
just before it disappeared.

For several days now Selina had found herself in the unac-
customed position of playing follower to someone else's
leader. Bonnie possessed the uncanny ability to think about
one thing while she talked about something else. Since Bonnie
was always talking, she was always thinking, always one step
ahead of her own mouth and the rest of the world. Selina,
who could barely think while Bonnie chattered, never had a
chance to make her own plans for the expedition to Eddie

Lobb's apartment. Once Bonnie got rolling, Selina had the sense that she was a lap behind.

Of course, she could have said no, or Catwoman could simply fail to show up outside Bonnie's apartment at the appointed time. She could have seized control anywhere along the way. She could have ignored the torrent of words and taken her own action. Bonnie was a steamroller, not a tank; the differences were significant. But Selina had not seized control, and Catwoman was going to visit that tiny uptown apartment before she visited the Keystone Condominiums.

Because Bonnie was good. Her plan for dealing with Eddie's collection was better than anything Catwoman would have come up with on her own. And her photography—

Catwoman paused to look at the Lucite-mounted photograph dominating the corner where she did her exercises: a sleek black panther drinking warily from an autumn forest stream. The panther reminded Selina of Catwoman. The forest reminded her of the woods not far from her parents' house where she'd hide when things got unbearable. Of course, black panthers weren't native to North American forests. Bonnie described—at great length—how she'd photographed the stream while hiking in Canada and the panther at a zoo, and then combined the two.

"It's not real," Bonnie had explained when she noticed Selina staring at it that first night while they sat on the floor eating take-out food. "The camera can't lie. It's not like your eye or your brain. It sees exactly what's there. Bars on the cages, garbage on the banks of the stream, telephone poles growing out of your grandmother's head. I think like a camera when I'm holding the camera, then I go behind closed doors and mess around with reality."

Selina wanted the picture. She was trying to think how Catwoman could get it, when Bonnie yanked it off the wall.

"Here, take it—it's yours."

Selina had held her hands tightly against her sides. Accepting a gift was not her style. Gifts made debts and obligations. She preferred to live without debts or obligations. But life did not always go the way one preferred. In costume, poised on the windowsill and looking back at the picture, Catwoman recalled how her hands had tingled. "It's just a photograph," she'd said, working herself up to take the gift. "I bet you made a lot of them."

Motormouth Bonnie had been taken aback. "No. I only make one. I even destroy the negatives. One's a dream; more than one would be cheating. But this is your dream. I saw it in your face when you looked at it."

Now the picture hung in Selina's room—very nearly the only thing not stolen, scrounged, scavenged, or purchased secondhand—and Catwoman had a partner. She descended the fire-escape ladder that went past Bonnie's apartment and scratched the glass with her claws. Bonnie came running out of the chipboard enclosure that united her kitchen and bathroom into a single, well-equipped darkroom. She was dressed in baggy, dark clothing with an army-surplus web belt slung low around her hips and well-used hiking boots.

Both women were surprised. Catwoman had expected to find Bonnie in L.L. Bean pastels. When Catwoman was surprised, she was quiet, but Bonnie started talking before she got the window unlocked and opened.

"The fire escape. I should have known. I mean, I shouldn't've expected Catwoman to ring the bell. That was silly. Standing there, listening for the doorbell and nearly jumping out of my skin when I heard scratching at the window. I'm almost ready. Do I look all right?" She retreated from the window and spun around like a little girl at her first ballet recital.

Catwoman nodded.

"I thought: surveillance, urban guerrilla spy versus spy stuff—I'd better dress appropriately. I've got real camouflage for photography, but it's all orange-blaze. Great in the outback, but silly here in the big city. So I just went dark, and matte, on account of light. Do you have any idea how much ambient light there is at night in this city, Selina? It's never really dark—well, maybe in the back of alleys and places like that, but on the sidewalks, you don't even need to use flash. I've got my flash guns, though. No telling what sort of light we're going to find, right? Two cameras, extra film, extra flash, extra batteries. It's all right there.'' She pointed at a dark nylon backpack on the sofa. ''Check it out—tell me if you think there's anything I've forgotten. Like a tripod. You've been there. Do you think I'll need a tripod?'' She reentered the jury-rigged darkroom. ''I'm almost ready.''

Catwoman let out the breath she'd been holding. Had she heard Selina's name, or had she imagined it? She'd told Bonnie outright, whenever she had the opportunity, that Selina, who'd come to the Wilderness Warriors, and Catwoman, who would get Bonnie and her cameras inside Eddie Lobb's apartment, were not the same person. Catwoman was one of Gotham's costumed characters, and Selina Kyle simply knew how to get in touch with her.

The laws of the universe affirmed that adult human beings tended to believe whatever they were told, but Bonnie had some distinctly un-adult characteristics. Maybe the laws of the universe didn't apply to her.

Catwoman shrugged and gave the contents of the backpack a cursory glance. Professionally she recognized a couple thousand dollars' worth of equipment, but she already knew that Bonnie's family had money and that they lavished it unstintingly, along with love and optimism, on their only child. Bonnie wasn't spoiled, not in the way Selina thought rich kids were spoiled; she simply assumed she was destined to succeed.

When the world slapped Selina down, she felt shame and humiliation. When it slapped Bonnie around, Bonnie blithely assumed that the world had made a mistake and would correct itself at the earliest opportunity.

Leaving the backpack alone, Catwoman moved stealthily to the doorway to see what Bonnie was doing. She was standing in front of a mirror wrapping her hair in a dark print scarf. When that was completed, she began smearing black goo across her face.

''It's the stuff football players use—you know, those war-paint lines they make on their faces. Especially the quarterbacks. Do you realize that war paint and camouflage are essentially the same thing? Anyway, I got it from my room-mate's boyfriend. He thought it was funny that I'd want to use it while I was hiking, so he stole a whole thing of it from the locker room. Wow—that's special! He stole it from the locker room, now I'm using it to steal from this Eddie-guy—"

"We're not going to *steal* anything," Catwoman heard herself say. "We're just going to take a few pictures and get out."

Bonnie gave a final swipe to her cheek and turned around. "We're stealing his secrets, Selina. What more could we take? Things can be replaced, but not secrets."

They stared at each other. Catwoman blinked first.

"Why do you keep calling me Selina? I'm not Selina Kyle. She's just someone . . . someone I know."

A long silent moment passed while Bonnie examined the black-clad woman facing her. Except for her eyes, no part of her moved. But the green eyes took everything in, slowly, methodically, and when they were done Catwoman had an entirely different opinion of innocence.

Bonnie swallowed everything she had seen. "Yeah, I un-derstand now." She nodded several times, affirming some-thing to herself. "Catwoman. Not Selina. My mistake. We don't have people like you out in Indiana, you know," she said, as if that explained something important. "I mean, we see the news on television and all, but nothing interesting enough happens in Bloomington to make it worth your while. So I had no idea how you do what you do. I thought it was like acting, playing a part—but I see I was wrong. You're not anything like Selina Kyle. You're Catwoman, pure and simple, right? And I better not forget it if I know what's good for me, also right?"

Catwoman stepped aside. Her mask was no better at hiding things than that guileless shrug and smile. Bonnie was, after all, the young woman who had spliced a black panther into a forest of pine trees and sugar maples.

"I'm ready if you are," Bonnie called from the window.

Catwoman led the way. She had to help her companion in the more difficult passages, but Bonnie understood—without being told—that this was a time for obedience, not conversation. She carried the heavy backpack without complaining, she did exactly what she was told to do, and she didn't say a word until Selina had them inside Eddie's empty apartment.

"You?" she asked, pointing at the gouges in the door and frame.

With a quick nod of her head, Catwoman bent down and went to work on the lock. It was a delicate chore; she'd damaged the mechanism on her previous visit. Hadn't Eddie been back since then? Finally the tumblers fell into place and the bolt could be drawn. She flipped the light switch and, despite knowing what was there, her heart skipped a beat. Everything was as she remembered it. In the pit of her heart, she believed that no one had been in the room since she'd left it.

"Omygod. Omygod." Bonnie hesitated before crossing the threshold. "Omygod. They won't believe it. Wide-angle won't be enough. I should've brought the camcorder. This needs movement, a slow pan across the entire room to make the eye see everything that's here. And slow freezes starting there . . . or there . . . or . . . Omygod. I don't know where to start."

"Just point and shoot. You're sure to get something illegal. There's a piece, a Siberian tiger box, in the room where we came in. Save a shot for that. I'll take a look in the other rooms to see if there's anything else we should have."

"Just point and shoot," Bonnie repeated. "Point and shoot. Omygod."

She unbuckled the backpack and opened it. When Catwoman left the room, she had both cameras on the floor beside her and was pulling on a pair of lightweight kid gloves. A moderately thorough search of the rest of the apartment assured Catwoman that except for the jewelry box in the bedroom there was nothing outside the now-unlocked room worth photographing. She was also positive that Eddie Lobb had not been back. This made her irrationally uneasy. If Eddie had been gone this long, there was no reason to think he'd be coming through the door any time soon. But reason had no effect on the acid churning in her stomach. She returned to the cat room to tell Bonnie to hurry up. Bonnie was standing on the tiger-bone chair, removing one of the trophy heads from the wall.

"Stop that!"

Catwoman was much stronger than Bonnie. She effortlessly wrenched the head from the other woman's hand and slapped it back on the wall.

"Don't touch things like that! What else have you touched?" Glancing around, Catwoman could answer her own question: everything on the right side of the room was subtly out of place.

"I've done the wide-angle shots in high-speed color; now I'm going for the close-ups in low-speed black-and-white. I'll get great enlargements. I've got to move things if I'm going to get good pictures. I'm wearing gloves. It's not like I'm leaving fingerprints around. Besides, I've never been arrested. There wouldn't be a match on file."

"But he'll know someone's been here."

Bonnie grimaced. "One look at that door and he's gonna know somebody was here, don't you think? 'Course, he won't know who, and he won't dare call the police—'cause if they came and saw this stuff, he'd be in heaps of trouble. Look, I know you said we shouldn't take anything, the proof's all got to be in the pictures, but it seems to me that—since you've already done a number on his door—we should go ahead and shake him up a bit. Move things around. I mean, a guy who has a room like this, he's got to be an animist. I'll bet he thinks these things have *mana*. You know, he sits here in his tiger-bone chair, works at his tiger-bone table, surrounds himself with tiger stuff. I'll bet he thinks he *is* a cat. Well, not like you're a cat, of course. But, anyway, he'll go loony tunes if he thinks somebody's messed with his stuff. I mean, I bet he'll really freak. He'll start thinking all these cats are turning against him."

"You think so?" Catwoman said slowly, chewing on a

steel claw. Bonnie had a habit of saying things and using words that didn't make a lot of sense to someone who hadn't paid attention in school. Animation? What did cartoons have to do with Eddie Lobb? But, as had happened before, Catwoman liked the conclusions Bonnie reached. "You think he'll get real upset if we move things around?"

"Yeah. Wait. I've got a better idea. Instead of just moving them around, we'll move them around in a pattern. See how he's got everything so it's looking down at his desk here? Well, let's make them look someplace else—the door. The door where you made those scratches. Like all the tigers turned their heads to see you walk in. Oh, it'll be great. I wish I could see his face! I mean, we will see his face eventually, 'cause these pictures are going to make everybody at WW weep blood. I promise you. They'll call lawyers, judges, all kinds of people. This Eddie Lobb guy—by the time we're done with him, he's gonna wish he'd never been born."

Catwoman wasn't listening. She was busy following Bonnie's suggestions, turning all the heads toward the mutilated door once Bonnie had photographed them. It was taking a long time, but it would be worth it. Then Catwoman heard sounds coming from the front door.

Mother of midnight—Eddie Lobb was coming home!

Bonnie was already packing her cameras. The midwesterner's eyes showed white all around and her breath was coming in panicked little gasps, but she managed to keep moving. Catwoman knelt beside her, passing lenses and film canisters in rapid succession.

"I'm scared," Bonnie whispered in the smallest possible voice.

"You'll be fine," Catwoman hissed as the apartment echoed with the sound of a metal bolt withdrawing from a metal socket. "Go down the hall, get out the window. Go to the fire escape and climb to the roof—just the opposite of how we got in here. Can you do that?"

Tears dribbled out of Bonnie's eyes as she nodded solemnly.

"Go. You'll be fine. Wait for me."

Catwoman turned off the lights, pulled the door shut, and guarded the hall. A second lock chinked free. They still had time. Nobody, not even Eddie himself, could get into this apartment quickly. She heard the drapes rustle and an involuntary yelp as Bonnie went out the window. Neither sound was loud enough to penetrate the living room. Catwoman held her breath, waiting for another sound, hoping it wasn't the sound of something heavy hitting something hard. It wasn't. She started moving backward down the corridor. She was in Rose's bedroom—damn, they hadn't gotten a picture of the Siberian tiger box that had started it all—when the front door opened. She was scuttling along the ledge below the window when it shut.

She caught up with Bonnie on the roof. The neophyte was slumped against the wall, quivering with terror.

"Hey—it's over. It's all done." Catwoman tried to pull her to her feet, but it was like pulling lead. "You did good, Bonnie. I know you got enough pictures to—what did you call it?—make them weep blood." Still no response. "Can't you see him—he's standing right in front of the door. He sees the scratches. He tries to open the lock. He's having trouble, getting nervous, he drops the key—"

Bonnie raised her head and grinned weakly. "Sure would be something to see his face when he turns on the light, wouldn't it? Zap him with a flash. Gotcha, Eddie Lobb!"

It was tempting. Very tempting. With Bonnie safe up here, Catwoman could easily slip back down with one of the cameras.

"They're not that hard to work, right? Just point and shoot?"

"Not quite, but almost. Here, I'll show you. Let me put a new roll of film in, too. . . ."

Moments later, Catwoman was headed back down the fire escape.

"Good luck!" Bonnie whispered after her.

It was a strange, warm feeling to have someone wishing her luck. Catwoman squelched it quickly. Luck was not something she liked to rely on.

Eddie was in the cat room. Catwoman could hear him yelling before she climbed through the window.

"Well, *cancel* it, I'm telling you. Screw the damn Bessarabs and their dirty pictures! I'm telling you, somebody broke into my place while I was gone."

Catwoman crept to the bedroom door and peeked out. She could hear him pacing as he talked, and she remembered that there had been a cordless phone on the table that Bonnie had moved to the floor.

"Well, let 'em stand there. It'll do 'em good to get a little nervous. I already heard that they've been lightin' up the town and getting everyone nervous. Do the greasy little sheep-herders good—"

There was silence; the pacing stopped. Catwoman understood that Eddie was getting reamed out by his boss. The warm feeling bloomed under her heart again, and this time she let it simmer.

"Yeah, right." The voice was subdued, the pacing slower. "208 Broad, off Tenth, in an hour. Yeah, I'll be there." Another pause, not as long as the previous one. "No, I don't know if they took anything. That's not the point. The point is some sick-o, punk bastard got into my place and messed around with my things, you know, boss, my *personal* things .. . No, no—not the front door . . . Shit, I don't know how— Rose . . . ? Shit, no. Maybe. I didn't look."

Catwoman hurried down the hall. She wanted his picture with the tiger skins in the background. She held the camera in front of her like a weapon or a shield, her finger poised above the button Bonnie told her to push and hold.

"Gotcha, Eddie Lobb," she snarled from the doorway. He was at least five feet away; Bonnie said the camera needed five feet if Eddie and the background were both going to be in focus. She pushed the button. Strobe-light flashes burst from her hand. Eddie was transfixed. His mouth gaped, the phone fell from his hand.

"A cat. Jesus H. Christ, it's a giant freaking black cat."

But he didn't move. Catwoman had no trouble making her retreat.

"He's one ugly dude," she said, giving the camera back to Bonnie. "He's got scars like the ones I put on the— Well, you'll see them when you get the pictures developed."

Zippers zipped and buckles buckled, Bonnie announced that she was ready to go home. They could look at the black-and-white pictures in an hour, when she had them developed. The color shots would have to wait until morning.

"Can you get home by yourself, kid? I'll help you get down to the street, but, there's someplace else I've got to go. . . ." 208 Broad off Tenth in an hour, but there was no need to tell Bonnie that.

Bonnie wilted, but she didn't whine. "Yeah. I think I'll take the bus, though. You'll—you'll tell Selina to get in touch with me, so I can show her the pictures?"

"Yeah, kid. C'mon."

CHAPTER
Thirteen

*T*HE night was warm, with a hint of summer's humidity in the haze. Batman traveled crosstown the hard way—without using the streets or sidewalks, just roofs, alleys, and basement tunnels. It was good practice, especially with a heavy wooden box clamped under his arm.

He was careful with the box, but not as careful as he would have been if he hadn't examined it thoroughly and made a few adjustments. Nothing that was visible on the surface— but then, what he'd changed had been well-hidden in the first place. The icon he'd received from the young man in the Russian bakery had been far too ordinary to be the major payment in a bartered-arms deal. The frame wasn't gold, but thinly gilt wood. There had to be something more, so he'd subjected the icon to close scrutiny in the Batcave, and found the real icon, the seventeenth-century masterpiece, sleeping under a removable veneer.

Bruce Wayne, of the Wayne Foundation, patron of a hundred useful causes, summoned the appropriate curator from Gotham's finest art museum to his office. Saying he'd found the object in an old chest in the mansion's attic—where wonders and trash had been found many times before—Bruce flicked the box open as if it were just another flea-market curio.

The woman dropped to her knees in awe and for a closer examination. She was speechless for several moments. She mentioned a name that meant nothing to Wayne and showed him where the artist had concealed it in the goldwork. She hoped the Wayne Foundation wouldn't consider selling it for less than three million dollars or before her museum had an opportunity to make an offer.

Another piece of the puzzle fell into place.

When Bruce Wayne was alone again he studied the delicate, melancholy saint with her hooded eyes and glistening gold headcloth.

Put it back beneath the veneer? Allow it to flow from hand to hand, until the weapons were moving toward Bessarabia and Harry Mattheson disposed of the priceless artwork? If Harry Mattheson was the Connection . . .

In the end Bruce Wayne locked the icon in the Foundation vault and reinstalled the flexible veneer over another, equally worthless, plank of lacquered wood. This way, no matter what happened, when it was over, the Foundation would make certain that an object of reverence and beauty could not be perverted again. He thought about injecting a short-range transmitter into the frame, but did not. He'd follow the icon in person, until it reached the Connection's hands.

The rendezvous was set for midnight in the warehouse district not too far from the pier where Batman first spotted Tiger. He arrived twenty minutes early, climbing out of an abandoned steam tunnel into a restaurant's basement storeroom. He expected to have time to check out the immediate area, but the ethnic Russian was in another late-night eatery across the street, so he decided to get rid of the box first. They met in a reeking alley.

"You have got it?" The young man asked the obvious, took the box, and found a patch of relative brightness in which to open it. His relief was palpable when he saw what he wanted to see exactly where he expected to see it. "I will speak well of you to my people." He closed the box and glanced nervously at the street. "You will go now. Three men can keep a secret only after one has killed the other two. Benjamin Franklin; citizen class. The Gagauzi and the scar-faced man, they would not keep our secrets."

Especially not the scar-faced man, Batman agreed silently. The young man started toward the street. Batman called him back.

"This is the only time. No matter what happens, there can be no next time. Not if you want to stay in America. Do you understand me?"

The youth nodded and ran. Batman waited until the street, as seen from the alley, was deserted, then looked for a path to the rooftops. He hoped the young Russian did understand.

It was a little after midnight when the dark streets resounded with unintelligible shouts and snippets of conversation. Five men got in each other's way climbing out of a single taxi. They were in high spirits, laughing and waving at the taxi as it made a U-turn and headed back to more-populated territory. From his rooftop perch, Batman watched them take their bearings from a torn scrap of paper. They came up the side-walk, toward him, toward the doorway some distance below where the Russian waited with the icon. Batman guessed they were the Gagauzi—the Bessarabians looking to outfit themselves for war, the men Commissioner Gordon wanted to catch before the act, rather than during or after it.

The quintet came up the block like tourists, pointing out the sights to each other, carrying on animated conversation as if the Gotham waterfront were Main Street USA. Batman could not measure their effectiveness as rebels or terrorists back in Bessarabia, but here they were innocents, and he worried about them. He considered alternatives while, below, the uneasy allies exchanged greetings in Russian.

Batman was deep in thought when he heard the faintest sound behind him, near the place where he'd climbed onto the roof. The Gagauzi erupted in laughter; if the sound was repeated, Batman couldn't hear it. He took precautions, re-ceding into the shadows and adjusting the mask so his chin did not reflect the light. Listening to the Gagauzi tell jokes he couldn't understand, Batman kept a close eye on the waist-high walls surmounting the rooftop. Even so, he nearly missed the dark shape rise and disappear into the black asphalt covering the roof.

The intruder made no sound and cast no shadow, yet Batman followed its movement along the back wall to the corner, then forward along the side wall toward the street. It stopped in the corner opposite his own. Had he, himself, been spotted? Batman gathered his strength, rising into a crouch, balancing on the balls of his feet, prepared for anything. But nothing happened. The intruder had found a vantage point identical to his own. The intruder was waiting, just as he was.

Without warning, the Gagauzi began to sing. Four of them chanted words and rhythms that sounded remarkably similar to Native American music, but the fifth produced an eerie, droning sound from deep in his throat that sent an involuntary shudder down Batman's back.

Filtered through the almost inhuman chorus rising from the sidewalk, Batman heard what might have been a resigned sigh. He relaxed, no longer expecting an attack. There was only one, inescapable, conclusion: The intruder was here to witness the same transaction. The intruder was virtually invisible, which implied a mask and gloves—in short, a costume not dissimilar from his own. The Russian's words came back to Batman—*They will hire your enemies.* From this moment on, Batman's attention was divided, and his options were limited.

Catwoman seethed. Her teeth were clenched, her fists were tight enough to tremble, that infernal wailing grated painfully in her ears, and—not fifty feet away—*Batman* was hunkered down in the shadows, no doubt ready to play havoc with her plans.

The cape had given him away, although she knew it was mostly luck that had her looking in the right direction when he reacted to the wailing. Whatever the cape was made of, it waivered ever so slightly from the movement beneath it. And

how did she know it was Batman? She didn't, but of all the
things she could imagine hiding under a cape, Batman was
the worst, so she assumed it was he.

And she seethed.

Eddie Lobb belonged to her. She knew that nothing legal
was going to happen on the sidewalk below. And she knew
Batman well enough to guess that he'd gotten wind of it and
that he was here to stop it. Whatever Eddie Lobb had promised his boss, wasn't going to happen—in a big way. But,
dammit, Eddie Lobb belonged to her. She didn't intend for
him to think that all the costumed fates of Gotham had conspired and united against him. She intended that he look into
her masked face, and hers alone, until he recognized his
doom. For a moment, no longer, Catwoman wondered what,
exactly, she intended to interrupt. Some sort of drug deal?
An assassination? It didn't matter. All that mattered was
Eddie Lobb.

Batman didn't really matter. Let him do what he wanted,
so long as Eddie saw her first.

The seething stopped, her fists unclenched. She opened the
unreflecting wool sack and pulled out a coil of nylon rope.

Let him come over and try to stop her or, even, ask what she
was doing. She'd tell him. Maybe they could work out a deal.

She crept over to a ventilation pipe rising from the asphalt.
After making certain it was well anchored, she knotted one
end securely around it, then ran the rope back to the front
wall. Her plan called for getting the drop, literally, on Eddie
as he arrived, but the roof was much too high for free-fall.
She peered over the edge, mentally measuring the distance to
the pavement—about sixty feet. Then she carefully recoiled
the rope, wrapping it between her elbow and the palm of her
hand, counting by two with each revolution. When she
reached forty, she knotted a trio of loops into the rope and
laid the entire coil carefully atop the wall. Now the rope
would get her safely down to dropping height.

Across the roof, Batman shook his head slowly. He'd recognized Catwoman as soon as she moved toward the pipe.

He watched her stand in his full sight and fuss with the rope. He had a pretty good idea what she meant to do. Batman didn't count Catwoman among his worst enemies, and he would have liked to know how the Moldavians had managed to contact her, but stealing the icon was her kind of job.

Too bad. Considering what he'd already done to the icon, Batman might have been tempted to let her get away with it, but he wanted to follow the box to the Connection, not back to the Commonwealth of Independent States. He'd have to stop her. He figured he could wait until she started to move— no sense risking the noise of a scuffle, although it was hard to imagine that the Gagauzi could hear anything but their own wailing voices.

Indeed, they couldn't hear anything else, but the two disparate personalities on the roof heard a booming sound that quickly resolved itself into an automobile stereo system with its volume control set for stun. It was not a sound either expected to hear, and they tracked its approach down the avenue. It slowed. It became abruptly silent. Without acknowledgment, they both crept forward. They saw what they wanted to see: a solitary walker headed this way in the next crosstown block, but hadn't made the noise. That had come from a high-riding 4×4 rolling blind and mute around the corner.

Catwoman gathered her rope. Batman pressed his hand against the cement capstone on the wall, muffling the sound of the thermite with his gauntlet. This wasn't in anybody's script. Maybe the gregarious Gagauzi had sung the wrong song. Catwoman drew her legs up onto the capstones, then dared a glance over her shoulder. Their eyes met for an instant, and they could no longer pretend to be unaware of each other.

The Gagauzi sang. The 4×4 cruised closer. Finally someone, Batman guessed the young Russian, spotted trouble coming toward them. Then all hell broke loose as the windows of the 4×4 came down and shotgun muzzles pointed outward. From the roof it was possible to see the flash as the shots were fired, but not to know where they struck. But someone screamed. The 4 × 4 stopped, and a trio of lanky youths in red satin jackets got out on the far side. They were firing their guns as they came around toward the sidewalk.

Batman's options had been reduced to a single imperative: innocents were being slaughtered. It was time to go below. Snapping the filament into a pliable steel groove in his gauntlet, he vaulted over the capstone. The last thing he saw was Catwoman glowering at him.

Despite the billowing cape and the dragline, Batman dropped like a stone, as he'd expected. He was ready when his feet touched the pavement and the dragline began to recoil. For an instant—less than a second, less than a heartbeat—his body was going in two different directions; then the dragline whipped out of his hand and his knees bent to absorb his excess momentum. No gymnast dismounting from the high bar or rings could have stuck the landing better. The cape was still furling around his shoulders when Batman took his first defiant stride toward the gunmen. In his peripheral vision he could see that two of six ex-citizens of the former Soviet Union were lying on the pavement. Two more had panicked and run, but the last pair was fighting back, no quarter asked or given, bare hands and a particularly nasty-looking knife against modern firearms.

The Gagauzi would be a force to be reckoned with if they managed to arm themselves into the twentieth century, although it was Batman's self-appointed task to see that didn't happen. He advanced on the nearest satin jacket. The kid—he couldn't have been more than fourteen—pumped the gun and fired, aiming right where he was supposed to: at the yellow-and-black emblem on Batman's chest where the thin polymer armor was bonded to a sturdy layer of Kevlar. Batman didn't blink. The kid threw away his gun with a scream and headed for the 4 × 4. Batman let him go.

The kid's scream brought a momentary halt to the skirmishing. All eyes focused on Batman, then the remaining guns. The two Gagauzi were slack-jawed. They believed in ghosts and devils; they believed they were looking at one.

"Get out of here!" Batman yelled. He had to believe this

was all an accident, a twist of fate. A culture clash between the sheep-herding Bessarabians and the drug-dealing Gothamites. If the police came now, Gordon would be ecstatic, but Batman would be as far away from the Connection as ever. He surged forward. The cape billowed as if he were chasing pigeons. In a way, he was.

"Scram!"

The combatants separated. Everything was going well, then one of the Gagauzi looked over at his fallen comrade, at the velvet-covered box lying unattended on the concrete. He veered, and the satin jackets moved faster. Batman *knew* the contents of the box weren't worth risking anything for, and it slowed his reactions. He got his hands on the satin jacket after the jacket's wearer got his hands on the box. The youth thought fast; he heaved the box to another member of his team, who, in turn, tossed it to the kid in the 4 × 4. Everyone still on their feet moved toward the vehicle, which revved its engine and flash-flooded the street with its full panoply of lights. Batman felt the satin go limp in his hands.

The 4 × 4's wheels screeched as it roared down the street toward the piers with the Gagauzi in hot, but futile, pursuit. Batman threw the jacket aside. He checked on the downed men. It was already too late for the Gagauzi. It might be too late for the Russian by the time Batman carried him to the nearest hospital, but he had to try.

Across the avenue, shielding himself instinctively in shadow, Eddie Lobb—Tiger to himself and his professional associates—surveyed the scene with a heartfelt curse. He hadn't been happy from the moment he heard the Bess-arabs singing. The goddamned sheepherders didn't belong anywhere near Gotham City; they didn't belong in this century. But his boss wanted that painting bad enough to do the deal right here because all the principals wanted to visit America. His heart had skipped a beat when the dark 4 × 4 whisked by. He thought it was as bad as it could get when the first shot was fired. Then, insult to injury, Batman dropped in out of nowhere to mix things up beyond all hope.

When he saw the wooden box—*the* wooden box—sail into

the 4×4, Tiger wanted to throw up. None of this was his fault, but the boss wouldn't see it that way when he found out. The boss would ream him out six ways from Sunday and he'd still have to try to track down that priceless, ugly painting.

Nothing was going right. Not since he gave Rose the tiger-head box. Maybe he shouldn't have given a talisman away like that. She hadn't liked it anyway. Shit, she wouldn't touch it until he made her. Maybe the tiger spirit was testing him. Maybe if he passed the test, everything would start going right again. He better pass soon. There were headlights in the street again. The van was coming. He'd have to put his story together in a hurry.

Eddie looked around, making sure the Batman was gone, then started walking toward the lights.

Catwoman watched him get into the van. She pounded her fist against the cement until it was numb.

CHAPTER
Fourteen

*T*HE Connection watched the procession of digital read-outs on the control panel beside him. They were independent of the holograph and transmitted data continuously. Tiger had never guessed their existence. The street brawler always tipped his hand while he stood in the van's cab, waiting for the holograph to fill the back area. Telemetry couldn't read thoughts. That was and probably would remain impossible: a man's thoughts were too idiosyncratic to be worth deciphering, but emotions were simpler and universal. The Connection had been chipping away at the physical code of emotions, and if the telemetry could be believed, his lieutenant was a contradictory mass of dread and hope.

He punched a button that would save the readings for later study, then a second button to initiate the holograph transmission. One of the many monitors facing him flickered to life and filled with a reconstruction of an otherwise anonymous face the Connection had plucked out of a crowd several weeks earlier. Beams of ruby-red light touched the Connection's face and hands, establishing the feedback loops that controlled the holograph. Speakers hissed to life with engine and street noises, then Tiger stepped into the fluorescent illusion.

The first thing the Connection noticed was that Tiger's hands were empty, but as they were also behind his back, the technological wizard played dumb. "Well, let me see it," he said amiably.

Dread spiked but, interestingly, hope did not diminish. In human beings, emotions were not zero-sum phenomena.

"The sheepherders struck out, boss. They showed, but they didn't give it over."

"They refused to give you the package?" The Connection tapped a switch with his foot. The laser beams ceased. The holograph was on auto-mimic as the Connection's fingers raced over a keyboard. "Tell me what went wrong?" He initiated a subtle strobe sequence. Tiger would not consciously perceive the flashes, but he would feel the cumulative effect as stress and anxiety.

"Almost everything, before I got there. The sheepherders got hit by a drive-by. They drove up fast and blind, jumped out, and started firing, then jumped back in and drove off again. Maybe one of the southside gangs—who knows—I didn't recognize their colors, but they knew what they were looking for and they hit hard. I was too far away to make a difference—" Tiger shuddered as if he'd just received a mild electric shock, which he had.

"Do you intend to tell me that a handful of punk thugs has my icon?" The mimicry circuits kept the holograph's bland features calm and reposed, but the Connection's lips had twisted into a sneer. He had only agreed to this risky, harebrained deal because of the icon. None of the players, especially the hopelessly naive and fractious Bessarabians, understood the true value of the articles they offered in trade for arms.

There was sweat on Tiger's upper lip and moving along the ridges of his scarred face. "No." Another shudder. "No, I don't know. I couldn't see what happened to the box. I was too far away."

"You said it was a drive-by. The Bessarabians got hit. The

box was with them when you inspected the bodies or it was with the drive-by gang.''

''Or maybe the Bess-arab sheepherders double-crossed us.''

The telemetry went wild. More importantly, the monitor attached to the Connection's keyboard came to life as he opened a back door into the Gotham Police telex. The cursor flashed rapidly, the screen divided, and data began streaming on both sides, in opposite directions.

''Why would the Bessarabians double-cross us? What could they gain? They'd have nothing to show for it, would they? The Seatainers are moored five miles off shore. Those guns and Stinger missiles might just as well be on the moon for all the good they'll do our little friends. The Seatainers *are* moored safely, aren't they?''

Tiger's nod was quick, emphatic, and confirmed by the telemetry. That part—the easy part: enough munitions to sustain a small rebellion for a number of weeks—of the operation was under control, but the other more important part, involving the antique Russian icon, destined for an Asian collector's very private gallery and from which the Connection expected control of two percent of the Golden Triangle opium trade, was very clearly out of control. The split screen continued to stream data.

''There's something you're not telling me, Tiger.'' The Connection adopted a parentally cajoling tone while he divided his attention among his many monitor screens. ''What went wrong, Tiger? Tell me.''

''The Bess-arabs ran, boss. They scattered like—like the sheep they are. I couldn't follow them all. One of them could've taken the box. Or maybe it wasn't a drive-by. Maybe it was a planned hit. Maybe the Bess-arabs *do* have enemies here. How should I know. There isn't one of them who speaks English worth shit.''

Telemetry indicated that the truth had been uttered, but not—as television was apt to say—the whole truth and nothing but the truth. Random violence wasn't unique to Gotham City. The Connection's line of work took him, or his minions, into the world's worst hellholes. He'd had other deals go sour in just this way. It was part of the cost of doing business. You scrambled, you recouped, you put the squeeze on one drug gang after another until they did your dirty work and produced the stolen property.

Tiger knew this.

Then one side of the split screen halted. The Connection cleared and refocused the screen. He watched in realtime as a transaction began its journey to the central memory: Gotham Memorial Hospital. Ten minutes ago a twenty-one-year-old Soviet immigrant admitted in serious condition with gunshot wounds to the chest and abdomen. The patient had been brought to Gotham Memorial by *Batman*, who advised that another body—another Soviet national—remained at the scene. The police had been notified and a meat wagon had been dispatched to the address: 208 Broad Street.

The Connection rubbed his eyes and returned his undivided attention to his lieutenant. He could guess what had happened with a high degree of confidence, but it was always better to get a confession.

"One of the Bessarabians could have taken the box, or the gang, or someone else. Who else, Tiger? Who else could have taken the box with the icon in it?"

The Connection fingered a dial. A readout showed that the strobe flashes were quicker now, and even more intense. Tiger's pulse quickened immediately and his blood pressure soared. Veins throbbed across his forehead and temples.

"They're testing me, boss."

The telemetry fell like a rock. True confession time had arrived, and Tiger was experiencing the exaltation of truth. But the words weren't anything the Connection wanted to hear.

"The guiding forces are measuring my worthiness. I told you how somebody had been inside my place while I was gone. The inner door had been forced—these big scratches all across it—but none of the outside security had been breached. And when I went inside, they had all turned and were looking at me. And I called you up because I was real pissed, because I thought someone had been inside my place, messing with my stuff. And we were talking, and you said 'what about Rose?' Like maybe the bitch had come back. And you told me what I had to do. And it hit me when I walked out of the room: bright flashing lights, and the cat. A big, black cat. It called my name. I didn't understand, not at first. I thought something was wrong, but then, while I was going down to Broad Street I heard them inside my head, saying: Are you the one? Are you the Black Tiger? Are you worthy?

"It's a test, boss. I'm right on the racer's edge. There's so much power around me, waiting for me when I become the Black Tiger. And when I saw the Batman there. Like, why would he be there if the Tiger hadn't drawn him? Then I realized: He's part of the test. Batman's part of my test. I faced him down once already. Now I'm going to beat him—"

The Connection cursed once, mightily and silently, that he had failed to discern his lieutenant's previous encounter with the costumed character. The men and women, heroes and villains, shadow seekers and spotlight gluttons who faced the world in aberrant clothing were beyond the Connection's comprehension. He could predict them, when he had to, but understand them? Never. He didn't want to try. And although the moniker and holographic disguises he used might seem to place him within the men, villain, shadow-seeker category, Harry Mattheson resolutely refused to make the connection.

His moniker and *his* disguises were legitimate business precautions, not flights of fancy—like Eddie Lobb's unfortunate notion of tiger spirits. At times the brawler seemed to forget he'd gotten his distinctive facial scars from a car antenna after falling behind in his gambling debts. His faith in tiger spirits and transformations was appallingly sincere. And while the Connection did not understand the arcane processes that produced those costumed characters whose talents did in fact lie outside the normal human range, he was quite certain Tiger was not destined to be any more than the punk he'd always been.

Mattheson wrote Tiger's name on a piece of paper, then embellished it with question marks. The scarred man was still giving his interpretation of events and the inevitability of his transformation.

"It was that box you gave me. It pushed me over the top; the tiger spirit came to see if I'm worthy, but I made the mistake of giving the box to that bitch instead of putting it with the others. But I'm over the top now."

Tiger was over the edge, not the top. The scarred man was writing his own death warrant.

"Batman's my test, my final exam to see if I'm worthy to call myself the Black Tiger. When I've taken care of Batman, see, everybody will know I'm worthy."

The Connection tapped his pen on the paper. He wanted to believe everyone who wore a costume was as deluded as his lieutenant, but a man couldn't always have what he wanted. Batman was real. Batman considered Gotham City as his personal domain. Batman was near the top of the list of reasons why the Connection was careful to keep his hands clean and his face hidden.

He weighed his options. He could fry Tiger where he stood, pull back from the deal, and quietly accept his losses. Or he could give Tiger a bit more rope and let Batman hang him instead. He depressed the foot switch. The lasers struck his face and the holograph became directly animated again.

"I don't care about Batman or black tigers. I found you dying in a gutter, Eddie, and I can put you right back where I found you whenever I want. You have a job to do for me: get me that icon. Do whatever you have to do: double-cross the Bessarabians, find their mysterious enemies, squeeze the gangs, fight a duel with Batman—do whatever you want, but get me that icon."

The telemetry began flashing. The telltale tension of betrayal and deception had been detected. Well, that was hardly a surprise. A man who believed he was destined to become the Black Tiger would scarcely imagine that he'd spend his life working for someone else. It was hardly a threat, either.

"Monday morning. In the usual place, Tiger."

The Connection tapped the escape sequence into his computers and Tiger was alone.

Batman saw the police officer get off the elevator and head his way like a bear to honey. They made eye contact. Batman made a quick side-arm gesture, and the officer waited where he was. The surgeon to whom Batman was listening missed the entire transaction as he continued his recitation of the young Russian's injuries and prognosis. He'd lost parts of a lung, his liver, his intestines, and his stomach.

"A shotgun at that range does quite a bit of damage," the surgeon concluded unnecessarily.

"But he's likely to pull through?"

The green-clad surgeon winced and looked uncomfortable. "We've done a lot of work. We think we've repaired the worst of the damage and stopped the bleeding. But the risk of infection is high. We'll know better in a day or two." He backstepped, effectively ending the conversation.

The police officer started moving again. Batman promised that he'd call in the morning. He blamed himself for the Russian's sorry condition. In his effort to gain more information and land bigger fish, he'd allowed a crime to progress beyond the point where he had it stopped. He'd needlessly exposed a young man—an ignorant and naive and therefore innocent young man—to the naked danger of the streets. And, in the end, he hadn't learned anything.

"Batman?" The officer had stopped just beyond conversation distance. He was clearly uncomfortable with his assigned duty. "The Feds came and took the body, before we could identify it. They chewed up Commissioner Gordon pretty bad. Now Gordon wants to meet with you in his office. We've got to hurry. We had trouble finding you, and we're going to be late."

Gordon's office wasn't any place Batman particularly wanted to be, but to refuse the officer's invitation was to endanger a long-standing, but always delicate, relationship.

"Let's not be any later than necessary," he said with more enthusiasm than he felt, and followed the officer through the hospital.

He followed in silence. He held little hope that the meeting with Gordon would be productive, and that little was squashed when he saw a quartet of unfamiliar faces waiting with the Commissioner.

Gordon rolled his eyes as if to say he was powerless in this situation and that Batman had brought it on himself. Then the bureaucratic bloodletting began. Bruce Wayne knew when he became the Batman that many of the people he was trying to help—the regulated, publicly funded, overworked agents of law enforcement—would stand in his way at every opportunity. He accepted their resentment and their small-minded insults as part of the price he paid, but after the Fed chief began his fourth or fifth diatribe about "Besserb counterinsurgency" Batman lost his patience.

With tight-lipped politeness he explained that the corpse they had appropriated had been a Gagauzi while he lived—a Turkish-speaking Christian from the central highlands of Bessarabia. The young man in the hospital was an ethnic Russian whose grandparents had been relocated to Bessarabia by Josef Stalin in 1940. The drive-by shooting had probably been an unfortunate coincidence, but if it wasn't there was a good chance it had been engineered by Rumanian-speaking Moldovan agents whose interest in preventing the consummation of the icons-for-arms deal was intense and personal. There were, therefore, three discrete factions, all of whom lived in an area politicians referred to as Bessarabia, but none of them thought of themselves as Bessarabians.

The Serbs, Batman added, were fighting in what remained of Yugoslavia.

One of the Feds had the decency to take notes; the other three folded their arms in obdurate silence. Gordon tried to break the stalemate with levity.

"Oh, for the good old days of East versus West and one-size-fits-all black hats."

The Fed chief, who was not the one taking notes, wiped

his hands together as if they'd come in contact with something unclean. "You've compromised a major international counterinsurgency operation, Mr. Whoever-you-are-in-there. I'm not at liberty to tell you the initiatives involved, but we had our operatives in place, ready to interdict, when your grandstanding blew the whole thing sky-high. Now we're back to ground zero. The transfer never took place. We've wasted our time and the taxpayers' money. We're stuck up here hoping that the Besserbs"—he pointedly did not change his pronunciation—"will reestablish contact before they head back up to Canada and we've lost them."

Operatives in place? Catwoman? Catwoman a federal operative? Catwoman a *spy*? The notion was ludicrous, and yet she was the only one at the scene whose motives remained unclear. It made precious little sense, but, then again, the whole situation made precious little sense.

Batman stoically endured the scorn and veiled threats until the Feds had tired themselves out and left. Then he turned to Gordon. "I've got to stop them," he said flatly, without elaborating on which "them" he had in mind.

"I know, you did your best." Gordon sighed. "Not even you could be expected to unravel this mess in time. It's a whole new world out there, and we're just trying to keep the peace in Gotham City. The Feds are claiming preeminent jurisdiction. I'm ready to give it to him and just hope that there isn't more bloodshed."

"No, Gordon. I can get to the bottom of it—at least here in Gotham City. I've got the key." He thought of the icon sitting in the Wayne Foundation vault. "I can lure all the parties into one place, and when I have them there, I'll let you know."

Gordon started to argue, then thought better of it. "You know how to reach me. Be careful. To the Feds you're just another amateur vigilante. If they can't catch these—who did you say they were, Ga-Ga-somethings?—they'll be just as happy putting you out of business."

Batman thanked him for the warning and left.

CHAPTER
Fifteen

"*I*T'S not really in our mandate," the Director of Wilderness Warriors said between puffs on his pipe.

He was in his mid-forties and, despite the pipe, the neatly trimmed hair, and establishment-approved tweed jacket, he looked like he'd be more comfortable out in the park, wearing love beads and bell-bottoms, and singing "Give Peace a Chance" through a haze of marijuana smoke. This made his apparent reluctance to do something about the stack of photographs, with narrative paragraphs on the back of each one, all the more disappointing to Bonnie. She didn't trust herself to say anything or to pick up the photographs he'd returned to her for fear that she'd throw them in his face and wind up without a job. Jobs—even an internship like this that paid next to nothing and required a major subsidy from her parents—were very important to her generation. She expected her boss, as a member of an earlier generation, to be a freer spirit.

"It's very well done," the director assured her, picking up the stack again. "Very compelling. Something *should* certainly be done about this man. But I don't see where we're the ones—"

142

"If we're not the ones, Tim, then who is? Where do I send these pictures? I have to find someone who'll take matters into his—or *her*—own hands. Does somebody have to break into this apartment and do what's got to be done?"

The director gave Bonnie a sidelong glance and began tapping the paper rhythmically against his palm. "That could only result in negative publicity," he mumbled. "We could lose money. Can't do that." He tapped the papers a few more times before coming to a conclusion he was not about to share with Bonnie—at least not yet. "Can I keep these?" he asked; she nodded. "I've got a friend. An old friend; we haven't talked in years, but he might be able to do something with this. Hang tight, Bonnie. Let me see what I can do here."

He left the reception area, still bouncing the photos in his hands and muttering to himself. Bonnie uncrossed her folded fingers. They tingled painfully as blood flowed back to her white, numb fingertips.

So Tim had "an old friend" who might be able to help; she had a new friend who could break into any apartment. In an instant she had a warm, fairy-tale vision of a Gotham City where almost everybody knew somebody (or was somebody) who wasn't what they seemed to be, and everybody who knew a secret, kept that secret the way she'd keep Selina Kyle's Catwoman secret.

Selina had to be Catwoman. They were the same size and build. Their eyes were the same color. Their voice was the same and they shared many gestures and expressions. It was easier to believe that Selina and Catwoman were one and the same person than it was to believe there were two completely different people who had so much in common. Bonnie would keep Selina's secret because secrets were mysterious and exciting and Selina was the most exciting, mysterious person Bonnie could imagine.

There were other reasons for keeping Selina's secret—not the least of which was that neither Selina nor Catwoman had put in an appearance since the adventure in Eddie Lobb's apartment. All weekend while she developed the film and made the prints, she had been distracted by day with the

hope that a dark-haired woman in decrepit, thrift-shop clothes
would knock on her door. By night, Bonnie listened for the
sound of steel claws on the window glass.

Bonnie's disappointment was a palpable weight in her
stomach. She knew the world wasn't a fairy tale. She regularly surrendered her illusions when the harsh light of reality
revealed them to be fantasies. But she didn't *like* doing it.
She was prepared to accept that Selina would never show up
again, just as she was already preparing herself to accept that
Tim would hand her back the photos and his regrets that his
old friend couldn't do anything about Eddie Lobb. But they
would be bitter pills to swallow, and she'd put it off as long
as she could.

All day she waited for the director to appear with a big grin
on his face, or for Selina to scowl into the security camera.
The director left early, without saying a word. Everyone else
left at five, and shortly after six Bonnie got ready to leave
herself. Feeling as lonely and miserable as she'd felt since
she'd waved good-bye to her parents, she gathered up her
"Warriors"-emblazoned coffee thermos and ecologically
correct reusable lunch sack and stowed them in a matching
canvas bag along with a mangled copy of the morning newspaper, refolded to expose the completed-in-ink crossword
puzzle. The extra set of photographs—the set she'd hoped to
give to Selina—had never gotten out of the bag.

The weight in Bonnie's stomach began a nauseous decom-
position. She sat down heavily in her chair, chiding herself
for this sudden plunge into misery.

It's not like we had anything in common, she told herself.
*Selina dresses like she lives in an attic, and Catwoman's
really just a criminal. She had me breaking and entering.
Me! I could've been caught. My life would've been ruined.
It's better I never see either of her again. We had an adventure
together, that's all.*

The pep talk didn't work; the heartache and disappointment
were too fresh. But they'd work eventually, and, confident
of that, Bonnie hung the canvas bag over her shoulder. Lock-

ing the Wilderness Warriors' door each night was Bonnie's responsibility, and she did it with great care, double-checking everything before she permitted herself to turn around and look at the sidewalk.

"You really should pay more attention to what's going on around you."

"Omygod." Utterly startled, Bonnie staggered away from the door and the voice. Her eyes said "Selina" but the rest of her was caught up in terror. "Omygod." The bag slipped from her shoulder. The straps tangled around her feet and she wound up sprawled on her rump against the garbage cans.

Selina held out her hand. "You're a smart lady, but you sure don't belong here in Gotham City." She easily pulled Bonnie to her feet, then hung the bag back on her shoulder. "You've got a nice home, nice family in Indiana. Why on earth did you ever come to Gotham City?"

"Why does anyone come to Gotham City?" Bonnie replied rhetorically as she brushed herself off. "This is where the excitement is. With all that niceness, Indiana's terminally boring."

Selina had nothing to say. She and Bonnie didn't actually come from different worlds. In all the little towns like the one Bonnie was from, there was a downwind neighborhood where the children of the town's losers grew up to become the next generation of losers. Selina came from such a neighborhood. Bonnie, on the other hand, lived on the hill with the respected folks. The only time respected folks saw the losers was before Christmas when a church delivered a twenty-pound ham with all the trimmings to the Kyle family's ramshackle front porch.

Selina still hated ham. She wanted to hate Bonnie, but the fire wouldn't catch،

"Did you get the pictures developed?" she asked with just a trace of hostility.

"I developed all the film and printed the pictures myself over the weekend. There were too many to be effective—that always happens—but you don't know which ones will work until you've actually got the prints in your hands. I thought about it a lot, and waited a lot hoping you'd come by, but finally, last night I picked out fifteen—''

"So you've given the pictures to your boss. Are the Wilderness Warriors going to do something, or are we S–O–L.''

"S–O–L?''

"Shit outta luck.''

Bonnie gulped air and nodded. "We're not S–O–L yet. Tim said he had an old friend who might be able to do something. *An old friend.*''

The extra emphasis triggered nothing in Selina's mind, and it was her turn to be confused. "I don't like getting other people involved. Can't you think of something else we could be doing?''

"We could be having dinner. I'm starving.'' She started walking down the side street toward the busier avenues. Selina followed. "And I suppose we could think of something else. Fallback plans. Contingency plans. Television! All the stations here have muckrakers. They'd love to get their teeth in a story like this. If Tim can't do anything, we could take the photos to one of the TV stations. It'd be great on TV. Of course, we'd have to break in again—with the camcorder. You've got to have tape—''

Selina took note of the steady stream of pedestrians on the avenue sidewalks. She wanted to hear what Bonnie had to say, but half the world would be able to eavesdrop on their conspiracy in another thirty yards.

"Yeah, let's have dinner,'' she interrupted. "Inside, at your place. We can talk there. Not while we're walking— okay?''

Bonnie agreed, and they got a bucket of flavor-of-the-month chicken wings from an establishment that didn't bear closer examination. While Bonnie clattered about in the dark-room looking for plates and napkins—"It's bad enough we've bought a bucket that can't be recycled,'' Bonnie said. "We don't have to compound the problem with paper plates and napkins''—Selina looked for the photographs in the canvas bag. She had to remove the newspaper first, and noticed the inked-in crossword puzzle—further proof, if any was needed, that she and Bonnie had nothing in common. She was about to toss it aside when an address caught her eye: 208 Broad Street. Unfolding the paper, she began to read.

It seemed that the gunshot-riddled body found in the doorway of that address was causing an international fuss. The man had been identified as Stepan Kindegilen. And those portions of the old Soviet Union now known as Russia and Moldova were demanding custody of the corpse. The two republics were hurling diplomatic insults at each other, the texts of which Bonnie's paper printed in full.

"Can you figure this out?" Selina demanded when Bonnie emerged from the darkroom with an armful of plates and cloth. "My eyes say English, but my brain says garbage."

Bonnie hunkered down beside Selina. She muttered something about bad translations, then sat back on her heels. "It's just a guess, but I don't think either the Russians or the Moldovans care about this Stepan. He wasn't supposed to be here. It says he didn't have a visa, but it doesn't say he's a criminal. Both sides are only interested in his corpse. Like there was something special about it . . ." Her eyes grew wide. "*Radioactive!* He's some poor soul from Chernobyl . . . Wait—Chernobyl's in the Ukraine. Where's Moldova? Where's my atlas—?" She crawled toward her stacks of books.

Selina grabbed her ankle. "Forget that. Suppose it was a box, about this big . . ." She made a frame with her fingers. "Maybe covered with old velvet. What could it be?" She remembered the object that had been thrown into the vehicle before it sped away.

A question had been asked, and Bonnie strove to answer it. She didn't consider any related questions, such as why Selina mentioned a box or why Selina was so interested in a handful of foreigners. Bonnie simply tried to answer the question that had been asked. She didn't have a photographic memory, but she did have a pretty good one, especially for things that others called trivia.

"Lacquer," she said after a moment.

Selina arched one eyebrow.

"Shiny lacquer boxes with bright-colored pictures," Bonnie elaborated. "I ask myself a question and I see an answer. Now I see a shiny box with a picture of a fairy tale on it. Somewhere I must've learned about lacquer boxes coming from Russia being valuable." She shrugged helplessly, as if the process was as mysterious to her as it was to Selina.

For her part, Selina looked down at the flawless crossword puzzle. She was on the verge of a conclusion when Bonnie snatched the newspaper away.

"Oo—wait. Not lacquer." She thrashed through the paper, making a mess, which, at least, was something Selina could identify with. "Icons. Icons—here. Look." She tapped her finger on a grainy photograph.

Bruce Wayne, the caption read, of the Wayne Foundation, had loaned the art museum a rare and priceless seventeenth-century icon. Mr. Wayne said he'd found the luminous portrait of St. Olga in one of his grandfather's travel trunks during a routine cleaning of his mansion's attics.

"Liar," Selina muttered on impulse, then noticed the searching stare on Bonnie's face. "He's just fronting for the police," she said quickly, not wanting to remain under the other woman's scrutiny. "You haven't lived in Gotham long enough, but the Wayne Foundation's always suckin' up to the city."

"Wow. I was going to go and see it. Maybe I shouldn't. Maybe it's too dangerous. But there aren't many examples of good seventeenth-century Russian iconography in the West. I really should go; it's a once-in-a-lifetime opportunity."

"Once in a lifetime," Selina said dryly. "You'd risk your life to see this picture. You must really like these things."

"No, I've never seen one, but this might be my only chance, ever. Who knows, someday I might *need* to have seen one, and I'll remember that I had the chance but didn't take it. There'll be guards there. It's probably no more dangerous than taking the subway."

"Do you take the subway?"

"Well, no—but I will, at least once while I'm living here.

Don't you want to try to do everything and see everything that you can?''

Selina chose not to answer. ''I'll go with you to see this icon,'' she said instead. ''What about tomorrow?''

''I've got to work. Maybe after work. How late is the museum open? What does the paper say?''

''Ditch the Warriors for a day.''

Bonnie's lips formed a silent O of surprise. ''I can't do that. It's my job. They count on me. I open the door. I answer the phone, open the—''

''Just once.'' Selina grinned. She had Bonnie cold this time. ''Ditch the Warriors, for the experience of it.''

''You're right. Of course you're right. It won't be too dangerous. There'll be guards there to keep the icon safe. They'll keep the people safe, too; why else put it on display in the museum? Right? Bruce Wayne—or somebody else— wants people to come look at it, right?''

Right, indeed, Selina said to herself.

There were guards posted at the doors of the hastily re-arranged gallery, and several mingling through the steady stream of visitors. All but one of the guards were longtime employees of the museum; the odd man, at Bruce Wayne's insistence, was an employee of the Wayne Foundation. He was, in fact, Bruce Wayne himself with a frosting of gray in his hair, cheek pads and nose pads, and bits of latex here and there to give him the unmistakable air of an unhappily retired city cop.

Ceiling-mounted cameras were taping everything, but Bat-man wanted to mingle with the crowd. He trusted his own ability to separate the sheep from the goats, if the sheep or the sheepherders should happen to wander through. He'd certainly recognize Tiger, whom he expected would put in an appearance. He hoped he might be able to pick Catwoman's mundane face out of the crowd as well, but he could have done all that from a comfortable chair in the security control room.

No, the reason Bruce Wayne circled endlessly around the

glistening icon was that he expected one of the interested parties to approach him with a conspiracy. And the reason he expected this to happen was that he'd submerged himself completely in the criminal mind. Walking his lazy circles, he radiated boredom, corruption, greed, and other twisted virtues of the demimonde. No one asked him about the object on display or the way to the nearest rest room. Honest folk distrusted the aura he projected. In the few hours since the gallery opened, he'd been plied four times with hypothetical questions about the security setup. The third time it had been a couple. The woman hadn't said anything, but she was the right size for the black cat suit. He'd remember her if he saw her again.

The Gagauzi made their appearance at midday, a close-knit quartet that never shuffled forward to get a good look at the icon. They gestured at the cameras, the velvet ropes, and the icon itself, arguing loudly in their incomprehensible language. Complaints were made. Bruce joined two of the museum guards in escorting the foreigners out of the building. He hovered nearby, asking if there wasn't something he could do to help, broadcasting his assumed criminality. They were nervous and suspicious. Their cultural signals were at odds with Gotham City. No one was going to get close to them, including Batman.

Wayne fingered the two-way radio slung on his belt. The device was considerably more complex than ones his erstwhile fellow guards carried. He could have placed a call directly to Commissioner Gordon. At the very least, the Gagauzi were in the country without visas. Rounding them up would leave the arms deal dead in the water. And it would leave a lot of ends dangling. Batman grit his teeth and returned to the gallery.

Two women came in. His mental alarms went wild. The pair were young and animated, mismatched in clothing and manner, but this was Gotham City, and there were no rules. Either one could have been the body inside the black catsuit. He couldn't get close to them without drawing attention to himself. One of them, at least, was aware of him. Considering the Catwoman's independence, Batman took this as a positive sign that was reinforced when they settled down on benches in a less-crowded adjoining gallery, out of camera range. Batman kept an eye on them for a couple hours; then they were gone and he could only wonder if he'd missed an opportunity.

The man he most expected and wanted to see didn't show up until a half hour before closing time. Tiger elbowed his way to the velvet ropes. He stretched and leaned as far forward as balance allowed. Another guard got to him first and told him to contain his curiosity. Bruce Wayne intercepted him moments later. Tiger glared ferociously at the sight of a uniform, any uniform, crowding him.

"Some guys got all the luck," Bruce Wayne said by way of an introduction. His voice was as subtly and completely altered as his appearance. There was no likelihood that Tiger would connect him with Batman.

"Not me," Tiger replied, hesitating but not retreating.

"And to think that he found this in his attic." Bruce paused long enough for confident disbelief to register on Tiger's face. "Makes you wonder, though," he continued, "what else this Bruce Wayne fellow's got in his attic. If you know what I mean."

Tiger's face was transformed. The suspicion was replaced by slit-eyed thoughtfulness. He studied the guard, and he thought about the idea the guard had put into his head. "Yeah," he said slowly. "It does." Not that he believed for one moment that the icon had come out of Bruce Wayne's attic, but the museum had taken the bait easily enough. A wealth of possibilities unfolded in Tiger's mind, and were covered over again. He had other things to do right now.

Like getting that icon out of the museum and using it to get back in the Connection's good graces. Burglary wasn't his strong suit. The icon appeared to be sitting on top of a cheap fiberboard pillar inside a flimsy acrylic box. He couldn't see any security except for these middle-aged rent-a-cops. He knew he had to be wrong. He'd been wrong about the icon from the get-go. He'd never guessed the dark, morbid picture the Russian showed him wasn't the picture the Connection was buying. He thought the new, revealed picture was just as ugly and overpriced, but he could see the gold and the jewels and he knew he couldn't afford to make another mistake.

"You guys for real," he said to the guard still standing beside him, "or are you just for show 'cause the real security's somewhere else?"

"We're real," Bruce Wayne replied honestly enough. "They don't turn the gadgets on until the gallery closes, or you'd have tripped every alarm leaning over the ropes like that."

"They got a foolproof system, huh?"

"No system's foolproof—" Bruce said significantly, then he smiled. "Say, what's your name, anyway? I like you."

Tiger returned the smile. He liked the guard, too. He had a gut-level sense of compatibility and a confidence that they could do business together. Tiger didn't usually feel empathy toward strangers. He felt a heartbeat of doubt, which he shunted aside. The tigers were testing him. It was time to follow his hunches. "Just call me The Tiger. You wouldn't be thinking that maybe you could tell me some more about how it ain't foolproof? I could make it very much worth your while." The guard hesitated; that was good, Tiger thought, the guy shouldn't be too eager. "I'm looking at a lot of business comin' my way soon. I could use someone like you who knows about security and shit."

Bruce Wayne made himself look and feel nervous. He glanced around like a man with something to hide. "Not here," he whispered. "I gotta think about it, Tiger. Maybe later."

"Opportunity like this doesn't wait 'til later. You want in now, I let you in now. I don't want guys who gotta think."

"Then I'm in. I'm your man," Batman said with no further hesitation.

CHAPTER
Sixteen

*B*RUCE Wayne retreated to the guard's locker room in the basement of the museum. He made certain no one was watching, then used the customized radio to tell Alfred that the bait had been taken and he was going incommunicado. Alfred would handle everything for Bruce Wayne and Batman, even take care of Commissioner Gordon if the Batsignal went up. He would also be alert for any other, less conventional message Batman might need to send.

Then Bruce Wayne put on an ordinary shirt and trousers, loaded his pockets with the very best in fake ID, checked his appearance-altering makeup, and strolled onto the museum loading-dock to meet his new partner.

Tiger led him downtown to a sour-smelling bar where the light came from the neon signs proclaiming the varieties of beer on tap. Most of the patrons were crowded around the bar watching the basketball playoffs. The home team was winning by a wide margin, and this was a home-team bar. No one noticed a stranger when Tiger called for two beers at his favorite table in the back.

Sinking deep into his adopted persona, Bruce Wayne didn't blink at what he half saw and overheard. He was one of these lowlifes for a while; their world was his world, their rules, his rules. Batman did not exist, except as an enemy. Slouching in a bentwood chair with uneven legs, cradling a stein of cheap beer between his hands, a reconstructed Bruce was in his element and completely at ease.

They spent a beer or two exchanging bona fides. Or, rather, Tiger drank while his new friend talked. After pounding his chest with his fist and making veiled allusions to killjoy doctors and infernal pills, Bruce ignored the alcohol in front of him. Bruce made up his criminal history on the fly, snatching bits and pieces from Batman's memory. Tiger was duly impressed. But then, Tiger was a criminal and criminals were among the most impressionable people on the face of the planet. Each and every one thought he was the smartest goon in the room, the guy who knew all the angles, the guy for whom the rules did not apply. Criminals were also gullible. Every time Bruce Wayne flattered his companion's ego, Tiger became more deeply convinced that he'd found a henchman he could trust.

Gradually, as the night wore on and the beer continued to flow, Wayne was able to take control of the conversation. He traded information about the improvised security surrounding the icon for information about the Connection. But although Tiger readily admitted that he'd done considerable work for the mysterious middleman, it became clear to Bruce Wayne that Tiger merely did what he was told and had no notion of the Connection's long-term plans. In his mind he'd never believed anything different, but in his heart he'd allowed a brief flicker of hope.

Tiger drank heavily. Bruce listened attentively to everything Tiger had to say; there was always a chance that something truly useful would slip in. And Tiger, thinking he'd finally found an audience that understood and appreciated his talents, began to speak recklessly of destiny and transformation.

"Today's your lucky day," he said, shaking his finger at Batman. "You're gonna thank your lucky stars that you was standing beside that icon when I came in. You're gonna be a rich man. Important. You just wait and see. You're gonna say: thank you, Tiger.''

"I already have," Bruce said admiringly. "You've got connections.''

"Yeah. Yeah I have." Tiger sat up straighter. He looked at his watch and drained his stein. "Okay. We gotta go now. We gotta meet someone. You let me do all the talking, understand? Once I got you in, then you can talk, but you don't know the boss, so you don't do nothing when we see him, okay? You still got that napkin you drew on?''

Bruce shook his head. He'd destroyed the crude diagram he'd made of the icon security. Force of habit, he explained with a shrug. Tiger became agitated, demanding that he make another diagram quickly.

"It's your bona fides. The boss sees you know what you're talkin' about and that you can get him that friggin' icon, he takes you into the organization.''

"Are we going to see the boss?" Bruce paused with the diagram half-drawn.

"Yeah. Sort of.''

Batman completed the diagram with care and accuracy. He had to assume that the Connection was smarter than his lieutenants. He had to assume that a man who'd survived outside the law for a half-century could spot a ringer. At the moment the icon belonged to no one. If it had to be given up like a pawn in a chess game to get Batman into the Connection's organization, that was something Bruce Wayne could live with. Folding the napkin in neat quarters, he tucked it in his wallet and followed Tiger out of the bar.

They walked several avenue blocks side by side. Bruce began to wonder if the Connection had written Tiger off. The possibility had to be considered. The Gagauzi debacle in front of 208 Broad Street was enough to cashier a lieutenant in any man's army, but, even more, Tiger's constant talk about fate and transformation marked him as a man about to walk off the edge. Then Bruce saw an antenna-sprouting package-service van turn out of a side street onto the avenue ahead of them. It cruised to the curb and waited with its lights on and its engine idling. No one got out; no one got on. Through the layers of latex and disguise, Batman's senses came alive with anticipation.

Tiger spoke rapidly with the driver, who made brief eye contact with Bruce Wayne before releasing the brakes. Bruce stayed on the bottom step with the wind and pavement at his back, watching every move the driver made after Tiger withdrew into the back of the van. He didn't try to make conversation or co-conspiratorial alliances. From what he'd already seen, the Connection ran his organization on a need-to-know basis, and the driver didn't need to know anything about the stranger braced in the open doorway as he got the van up to speed.

Nothing could have prepared Bruce Wayne for the jolts and noise that struck the vehicle without warning. He needed both hands to keep himself from falling backward onto the pavement; there was no way to protect his ears from the assault. The torture subsided to a bearable shake and whine in less than a minute. Batman shook his head to clear it and caught a glimpse of the driver smiling smugly beneath his bright yellow protective ear muffs. He returned a toothy grin and hauled himself up the steps just in time for the partition door between the driver's cab and the cargo area to slide open.

"You can come in now," Tiger said.

The petty crook Bruce pretended to be was overwhelmed by the illusion surrounding him. He stood stock-still with his mouth gaping open while the real Bruce Wayne analyzed everything and committed it to memory. One technological wizard to another, he could admire the Connection's obvious genius. He couldn't see the cameras and sensors, of course; he saw the same holographic illusion Tiger did, but Batman was, perhaps, the only other person who could truly appreciate the genius that created it. Gradually, when he'd inferred all that he dared from the illusion, Bruce Wayne allowed the petty crook to take a hesitant step toward Tiger and the faintly glowing holograph.

"What is this?" Bruce Wayne asked with an awestruck

voice. He jabbed at the nearest apparent surface. His hand disappeared, as he expected. He pretended to panic and managed to fall through the illusion, gaining a quick look at some of the transceiving equipment before reinserting himself into the holograph. He did a credible imitation of a man whose worst nightmares had come true.

"Call it a rite of passage," the holograph said smoothly.

Bruce Wayne got up from his knees. No wonder the descriptions never tallied. A man who could create one perfect holograph could transform himself a thousand times over. On the other hand, the man who created this illusion was pumping a powerful signal into this van. It was undoubtedly disguised and encrypted, but it had to be real and it had to be detectable.

I've got you now, Harry. The thought rose irresistibly from Batman's consciousness. Bruce lowered his head and covered his eyes, lest the telemetry capture it.

"I told the boss that you can get the icon."

Bruce stood up and submitted to a thorough interrogation through the holograph. He produced the napkin sketch, wondering what provisions the Connection had for taking realtime information out of the van, or if he'd have to leave the flimsy paper behind for a delayed physical examination. He was told to put it on the holographic desk, where it floated half in, half out of the illusion. The Connection's holograph appeared to lean over the precise spot where the paper lay. Its eyes narrowed and its forehead wrinkled with simulated thought. Because he was watching, Bruce saw the red beam of an optical scanner move rapidly across the upper surface of the napkin; he also saw a similar beam shoot out of the floor to scan the reverse side. Bruce Wayne could imagine the Connection leaning over a display screen, watching the scanner reveal the sketch while another set of optical scanners recorded his own reactions.

The chess game between Bruce Wayne and Harry Mattheson had begun.

"I like it," the holograph said. "You've done this sort of work before." It was a statement, not a question. "How long will you need?"

"A couple days. By the end of the week. Next Saturday would be better. The exhibit's going to end then and the museum will be closed 'til Tuesday." By then Bruce Wayne could change the security completely, unless he decided to go ahead and give Harry the icon.

"Good. Leave a list of what you'll need with the driver. He'll get back to you—let's say, next Wednesday night, ten P.M. in front of the McAllister Theater—"

"Boss?" Tiger interjected with a worried, left-out look on his face.

"You've got to tie things up with our friends the Bess-arab sheepherders. They're getting desperate. Starting to make noise."

"But, boss, they don't got the picture. So they don't have the goods to complete the deal. So I've been telling them to go back to Bessarabia where they belong."

"They're not going, Tiger. You've got to be more persuasive."

Tiger cursed under his breath. "I'll persuade with lead right between the eyes."

The holograph scowled. Tiger didn't notice, but Bruce Wayne did. "What's the point here—getting rid of 'em or getting them to go home quietly? Tiger says you've already got two icons in the bag; I'm gonna get you the third one that you wanted—so what's the harm in giving them a little of what they came here for?"

And giving Batman the information about where the arms were stashed so he could get the word back to Commissioner Gordon, who would interdict the entire transaction.

"Yeah, boss—you're gonna get all your pictures. Maybe we could throw 'em a bone or two."

Bruce Wayne saw a red flash and felt a brush of an electronic scanner. No ordinary man possessed the reflexes to detect the subtle telemetry probe. To preserve his own illusion, Bruce exerted extraordinary control over his pulse and skin temperature.

"It's your problem, Tiger. You solve it," the Connection

said while the virtually invisible scanners continued to make their measurements. "I don't want to hear about the Bess-arabs again."

"You got it, boss. Me an' him," Tiger pointed at Bruce. "We're a team now. We'll take care of everything."

"You do that, Tiger. You do that and I will be very pleased."

There was a blinding flash of light accompanied by an electrical jolt. Bruce Wayne could not prevent his body from reacting protectively. He lost consciousness for a few seconds, five at the most, and when he came to the only light in the back of the van came from a dim fixture in the ceiling. Tiger was frozen in the grip of a petit mal seizure. Guessing that this was normal procedure and that Tiger had endured it many times before, he allowed his companion to recover in his own time.

Almost a minute passed before Tiger gasped and started breathing. He blinked several times and wiped the saliva from his mouth, but these appeared to be unconscious movements.

The first words out of Tiger's mouth were: "I sure can pick 'em. I knew that security stuff of yours was good when I saw it. The boss likes you."

"I'd hate to find out what happens when he doesn't," Bruce replied dryly. Every nerve was ringing like a bell or a rotten tooth.

"Don't worry about it. You and me, we're gonna work well together. You got smarts. He likes that, but you gotta be careful talkin' up the way you did. The boss don't like you to get ahead of him with ideas. He thinks he's got all the brains around here."

The van slowed to a stop. Tiger pulled a cord to open the rear access door. The two men stepped out into a dark, narrow alley. The van sped away. Batman recognized the angles of Gotham's Old Town, the twisted maze of streets where the city had begun almost three hundred years earlier. He would need a few moments to orient himself precisely. Tiger didn't need that long.

"I gotta take care of the Bess-arabs right away," he said. "Those damn sheepherders have been nothing but trouble from day one."

"Why did the boss bother?" Bruce asked innocently as he followed Tiger out of the alley.

"I dunno why he does anything, but he never does it the easy way. It's always a little here, a little there. I guess he wants those pictures for something else, maybe something real big. I don't know when a deal ends and another begins. Sometimes I think, maybe, he's playing the shell game. You know the shell game?"

Bruce nodded. "Except he does it with ships and paint."

Tiger paused before a metal door. Suspicion twisted his scarred face. "Yeah. He has the ships painted while they're out at sea. How'd you guess that?"

"Just lucky," Bruce replied easily.

Tiger hammered on the door until it cracked open and a sleepy Oriental face peered out.

"I want to talk to Khalki," Tiger said, thrusting his weight against the door to prevent the doorkeeper from slamming it shut.

They exchanged insults. Batman was not surprised to find that Tiger knew the coarser words of several languages. But the door finally swung open. Bruce Wayne thought he'd seen the worst Gotham City had to offer, but he wasn't prepared for the squalor inside the abandoned factory building.

"They pay rent by the square foot," Tiger explained as he wove confidently through the hivelike structure.

"Who are they? What are they doing here?"

"Illegals. We sneak some of 'em in along with everything else, but they come from all over—for the opportunity. These ain't the homeless or the unemployed. These are the cream of the fourth world. They all got jobs—and they're makin' more money than they could at home. They don't wanna spend anything on themselves 'cause they all got families at home they're sendin' money to. So they come here. Some of the old-timers make their money subleasing toilets. There's a friggin' waitin' list for this hellhole. What you see here, my friend, is the future of America."

There was no electricity, no water, no sanitation. Men—there were no women here—lived cheek-by-jowl in conditions worse than any antiquated prison. Most of them were asleep in cells no larger than the reeking mattresses they slept on. The little light came from candles and open-flame lamps. Bruce Wayne couldn't keep himself from looking into the cells, into the wide-eyed faces with their uncanny mixture of fear and hope.

The faces were timeless. Bruce Wayne had seen them staring out of hovels and boxes all around the world, coal mines and prison camps, nineteenth-century pictures of immigrants and fourteenth-century engravings of Black Death survivors. They were all steerage passengers on the ship of fools. He could barely contain his outrage. No man should live like this, and yet there was a measure of truth in Tiger's cynicism. Life in the subbasement of America held more opportunity and hope than life in much of the rest of the world.

Bruce was thinking about the drug-ravaged East End and comparing it to this when Tiger led them into what appeared to be a cul-de-sac.

"Khalki—open up." Tiger pounded the cheap wallboard until the dust billowed. "Dammit, you've been pestering me for days. It's Tiger. Open up!"

Other voices, awakened and angered by Tiger's shouts, joined the chorus. There was hatred here, held barely in check by the fear and the hope. Bruce Wayne hooked a finger over his collar and swallowed anxiously. If this place erupted, no one would get out alive.

Finally a panel swung down from above them and then a rickety ladder. Khalki and the three other remaining Gagauzi were hiding in the crawl space beneath the original roof. Bruce didn't want to guess how much they were paying for the privilege. He tucked his head and allowed himself to be guided to what he realized with some horror was a charcoal grill slung from ancient electric wires. Khalki, a clean-shaven man in his early thirties, offered him coffee and, without thinking, Bruce accepted. The other Gagauzi huddled close together on the far side of the swaying fire. One was a boy not yet out of his teens, the second was as old as Bruce was pretending to be, while the third was about his true age. At first he thought they were three generations of one family; then he realized that the resemblance was purely superficial, created by fear and strangeness. They stared at him while Khalki and Tiger conducted an animated conversation.

Bruce Wayne filled his mouth with coffee. It tasted burnt and sweet, with the texture of crankcase oil mixed with sand. The youngest Gagauzi stifled a smirk. And Bruce remembered the Gagauzi were ethnic Turks with whom coffee was an art, not a wake-up beverage. He gulped heroically and set the cup on the floor to precipitate.

"He wants to talk to you," Tiger said to Bruce after several minutes of apparently futile discussion. "Tell him he's got to do it my way."

"What is your way?" Bruce asked, getting cautiously to his feet.

"We meet day after tomorrow, midnight, Pier 23. We go out to sea. I give 'em what their pictures bought, we radio the freighter and put them and the merchandise on board. An' I never see their friggin' faces again."

Bruce nodded and began lobbying Khalki with words and gestures, just as Tiger had. The Gagauzi relented; he wanted to go home with whatever he could salvage from his nightmare. But before he led Tiger and Bruce Wayne back to the ladder, he rooted through his meager possessions and came up with a small enamel pin of a gray wolf on a red field.

"Gagauz flag," he said proudly as he affixed it to Bruce Wayne's shirt. Then he executed a military salute. "Hero."

All the way out of the firetrap, Bruce Wayne reminded himself what the Connection was doing was not right and what he was about to do was not betrayal.

It wasn't hard for Bruce to get away from Tiger for a few minutes. He crouched in a doorway and wrote a message to Alfred. He told the butler to contact Commissioner Gordon with the where and when of the arms. He paused and looked around; Tiger was nowhere to be seen. He turned the paper over and added a second message:

> Catwoman showed up at the museum. At least I think she did. Whatever her involvement with the icon has been, I don't want her showing up at the pier. I think you can lure her back to the museum. Try to intercept her and get her to go to—

Bruce paused. The possibilities were endless, but he could hear Tiger crunching through the rubble at the end of the alley. He took the location at the top of his mind—the place where Catwoman had left a message for him—and wrote it down. Then he scrolled the paper swiftly into a capsule the size of a disposable cigarette lighter. He sealed it and dropped it before Tiger got into hailing distance. In fifteen minutes it would send up a homing beacon.

Tiger was feeling much relieved. "How are your sea legs, old man?" he said, clapping Bruce roundly on the shoulder. "Hope they're good ones, 'cause we got a bit of sea work to do."

CHAPTER
Seventeen

*B*ONNIE coiled her feet around the legs of her folding chair. She was determined that she would not bounce, or leap to her feet, or do any of the other celebratory things popping in her head like soap bubbles. She would sit calmly in her uncomfortable chair with the serious look pasted on her face that she saw on the faces of the other Wilderness Warriors seated around her. After all, Tim's friend—who, it turned out, belonged to the Gotham City Federal Prosecutor's office—had made a special trip uptown with his charts and yellow notepads to tell them what he was going to do with the information the Warriors had provided.

It had already become apparent to Bonnie that she was not going to get her fair share of credit. At that moment, however, she was in sufficiently high spirits that the snub cast no shadow across her happiness.

"We're going to put the squeeze on Edward Lobb until he sings the right song," the extremely clean-cut lawyer said with a wolfish grin.

Edward Lobb was not a nice man. Bonnie had known this from the beginning, but the lawyer made it clear that Eddie's habit of collecting the bodily remains of endangered species paled beside his many other illegal activities. On the other hand, until Bonnie's photographs arrived in the Federal Prosecutor's hands, they'd been unaware of it.

"We like to target midlevel sleazeballs like Eddie. They take us up and down the ladder of their organizations," the lawyer explained. "We look for their Achilles' heels. Your pictures gave it to us for Eddie Lobb. We went to our judge; she gave us the search warrants. We'll execute those warrants tomorrow morning at eight A.M. We'll clean that place out. We're going to prove that every item in that room was illegally brought into this country, and we're going to throw the book at him for each and every piece. If Eddie's sleeping in, we'll have him, too. If he isn't, by noon we'll have arrest warrants printed with his name on them in letters two inches high. He's looking at death from a thousand cuts, until he cuts a deal with us."

Bonnie clamped her teeth together. She understood that this was the way American justice worked and that getting Eddie to rat on his associates from a witness protection program was more useful than simply throwing him into jail. She suspected that Selina, and Catwoman, were going to see things differently. She could, in fact, imagine the questions Selina was going to ask, and decided she better have the answers. She raised her hand and waved it.

"Do you have a question?" the lawyer asked wearily.

"What happens to the stuff in the photographs? Does Eddie get to keep that collection if he does what you want him to do? I mean, that doesn't seem right."

"No, ma'am, it wouldn't be right and we won't let it happen." The lawyer looked at Tim, then smiled. "I guess we can jump the gun here a bit, can't we?"

"You're in charge," Tim confirmed.

The lawyer rearranged his charts; a large blank sheet of paper faced outward. With courtroom dramatics, he tore off the blank sheet. Bonnie and the others beheld a mock-up of an announcement of a special exhibit at a major national museum: The Silent Victims of International Poaching, sponsored by Wilderness Warriors, Inc.

Tim got to his feet. "The museum's been looking for a way to make a statement about consumer responsibility in the whole illegal trafficking issue. We faxed them copies of the wide-angle photographs and they saw the statement they wanted to make. No matter what happens to Edward Lobb, that room's going to Washington. Visitors will see how much damage just one sick individual can cause. And, of course, they'll see our name and what we're trying to do to prevent it from happening again."

The news was too good for Bonnie to bear in polite silence. She leapt to her feet, clapping her hands.

"We won! We won!"

The others stared at her mercilessly, but Bonnie didn't care, even though she blushed furiously before she sat down. A little embarrassment couldn't hurt her, not when in her mind's eye she could see Selina's face when she told her the good news.

She was meeting Selina for lunch. Now that Selina had finally gotten her phone fixed, it was possible to call her. Inwardly Bonnie was waiting for the magic moment when Selina invited her home, but so far, although Selina had reluctantly parted with her telephone number, she would reveal nothing at all about where she lived. Bonnie thought about following Selina. It wasn't as if she knew nothing about stalking. Once she'd stalked a mother bear back to her den and gotten a whole roll of pictures of the cubs. Of course, she'd also gotten sent home from summer camp. The consequences of meeting Catwoman when she didn't want to be met might be a whole lot worse.

The lawyer droned on about the legal case he planned to mount against Eddie and the mysterious organization for which he worked. Bonnie was bored. She was reduced to watching the digital counters on her watch. Twelve-fifteen. If the meeting lasted much longer, she was going to be late. Finally Tim noticed what she was doing.

"Do you have to go somewhere?" he whispered.

Bonnie thought a moment, then nodded.

"Then go—you're making everyone nervous."

With a grateful smile, Bonnie hurried from the room. She paused by her desk to grab the morning newspaper—the original reason she'd called Selina and suggested they get together for lunch—then raced out the door. She was panting when she reached the restaurant at twelve-forty. She was ten minutes late; Selina was nowhere in sight.

"She's about my height with dark hair and dark eyes. She looks like she's real strong and she dresses kind of strange." Bonnie quizzed the waiter.

He shook his head. "Nobody's come through the door like that. I think I'd remember if I'd seen her."

It was another beautiful spring day. Bonnie accepted a seat at one of the outside tables, even though it was a bit cool. She figured Selina would be more comfortable in the fresh air. She didn't know her new friend well enough to know if Selina was always late, but she hadn't been early any of the other times they met. It didn't occur to her that Selina wouldn't show up until a neighborhood church rang a single bell for one o'clock.

"I guess she's not coming," Bonnie admitted to the waiter who took her order.

But before the soup arrived, a shadow fell across the table.

Selina vaulted over the empty flower boxes separating the café from the rest of the sidewalk. "I'm so late I thought you might have left already."

Bonnie squinted into the sunlight. She couldn't tell if Selina was sorry that she was late or sorry that Bonnie had waited. As a matter of fact, Bonnie almost couldn't tell if it was Selina Kyle standing in front of her. Her hair was trimmed fashionably short, her clothes were brand new and quite stylish.

"I got some money over the weekend," Selina said preemptively, pulling out the other chair at the table. "It was about time I got myself some new clothes. One thing led to another and here I am, late as usual."

"You look real nice—but so different. Are you comfortable? I mean, do you still feel like yourself?"

Selina's answer was a shrug as she reached for the menu. Bonnie felt foolish.

"I was late, too. But wait until you hear why . . ." And she began the tale of the morning meeting.

Selina cut Bonnie short. "What about the relics? What happens to them in all this?"

Smiling with satisfaction, Bonnie explained, "The whole room's going to Washington to be part of a museum exhibit. People will be shocked and, hopefully, they'll realize that they've got to do more to protect wild animals from the Eddie Lobbs of the world."

Selina sat back in her chair. The waiter came to take her order, giving her a few moments to think about what Bonnie had said. "Tomorrow," she said slowly, debating within herself whether she'd kill Eddie tonight, before the Feds came and carted his relics away, or after. Her gut preference was for after he'd lost everything, but the Feds would probably have him in custody by then, and they were notoriously unsympathetic to free-lance justice. "Tomorrow. I can live with that."

"But wait—that's not the only good part. Look at this!" Bonnie unfolded her newspaper and spread it across the table. "What do you think of it?"

A moment passed before Selina spotted the announcement in question, but once she did it held her attention.

Alfred had fulfilled Bruce Wayne's expectations. He'd retrieved the message cylinder and duly notified Commissioner Gordon of the upcoming exchange. That was the easy part. Contacting Catwoman and drawing her away from the scene had taxed his ingenuity. The fact that Bruce had seen Catwoman at the icon exhibit did not lead Alfred to believe that he could come up with an announcement that would lure her back, and even if she did return, that he could identify her. He could not look into a stranger's face and know if she were a cat burglar or simply someone who let things get moldy in the back of the refrigerator.

By the same token, the butler could not imagine letting his

friend and employer down. If Bruce Wayne wanted Catwoman lured away from Pier 23 at the critical time, Alfred
would find a way. Time had almost run out when Alfred
called the arts desk at the morning paper. Could they please,
as a favor to Mr. Wayne and the Wayne Foundation, insert
a small piece into the next City edition?

Selina could not know any of this, of course; she only saw
and read the final result:

> Are you one of the thousands who stood in line to
> see the icon at the Gotham Art Museum this week-
> end? Did you like the style, but not the subject?
> Then you'll be pleased to know that an anonymous
> gentleman is prepared to disperse his collection of
> secular icons—including the humpbacked horse, the
> firebird, miscellaneous legendary subjects and an ex-
> tremely rare series of cats. This offering is by ap-
> pointment only. For further details, please call . . .

The announcement concluded with a phone number.

"This is a joke," Selina said after reading the ludicrous
text for the second time.

"I thought so too, but I called the number anyway—just
to see what would happen. But it's for real, or at least the
man who answered knew what I was talking about. He asked
me if I was interested in a particular subject, and I said 'a
Catwoman,' naturally, and he gave me an address and then
said," she cleared her throat and deepened her voice for
effect, " 'Come at midnight.' Midnight! Like a real art gallery's going to be open at midnight, right?"

The food arrived. Selina found that she'd lost her appetite.
"Did you write down the address?" she asked coldly.

"I wrote it down. I've got it here someplace." She began
to rummage through her purse. When the quest failed, she
closed her eyes and recited an address in one of Gotham's
trendy, transitional neighborhoods. "When I write something
down, it's as good as memorizing it. I never forget. Honest.

Do you think it's somebody trying to make contact with
Catwoman? Is this how you usually do it? Should we go
investi—?''

Words froze in Bonnie's throat when she caught sight of
Selina's ice-cold eyes.

Selina rose from her chair. "You've gone too far," she
said. "This isn't a game, and you're not my partner."

"I'm sorry, Selina," Bonnie said quickly. "I didn't
mean— I won't—"

But it was too late. Selina had vaulted over the flower
boxes once again. She was putting distance between herself
and the café as fast as her long, muscular legs would allow.
The waiter saw her leave. He hurried over to the table with
the check in case Bonnie thought she was going to do the
same thing. Bonnie emptied her wallet and told him to keep
the change as a tip. She was on the sidewalk as quickly as
possible, but Selina was gone.

For the first ten blocks Selina was too mad to think. She'd
gone another ten before she began to think clearly. Not that
she liked any of the nattering thoughts swirling in her head
like wasps. Everything was Bonnie's fault for butting in
where she didn't belong. No, everything was Selina's own
fault, for thinking that she could let anyone inside her armor,
for thinking that she could have a friend. She was Catwoman.
That was enough. Catwoman didn't trust anyone, didn't need
anyone—certainly not anyone like Bonnie.

She'd gone thirty blocks by then, halfway between the
world where Bonnie lived on her parents' money and the East
End. Halfway home. And only about fifteen blocks from the
address Bonnie had given her, which Selina remembered
without writing down. It wasn't as if Bonnie was wrong; the
girl had, as usual, jumped to the right conclusion. Someone
was trying to send a message to Catwoman, which Catwoman
never would have gotten with only Selina to scout for her.
Only fifteen blocks, then she could look around and put everything behind her.

Even Eddie Lobb? her conscience inquired.

Selina stopped walking. She stared up at the clouds and forced herself to take long, steady breaths.

Yes, even Eddie Lobb. Everything would be finished, squared up, and cut off in fourteen blocks. She started walking again, a bit slower now, enjoying the sunshine and daring to think just a little bit about what she might do next. She zigzagged through the patchwork neighborhood where renovated buildings stood next to vacant lots and abandoned eyesores. She thought it looked familiar—but Catwoman prowled these transitional neighborhoods and they all looked familiar. Then she turned the last corner.

The scene was very familiar. The burnt-out drug house was on her right. The partially renovated building where she'd written her message for Batman was about a block away to her left. She didn't bother going the distance to compare the numbers.

"Damn you." She made fists and pounded them against her thighs.

Midnight. Bonnie said the man she'd spoken to—Batman himself?—told her to come here at midnight. So Batman wanted Catwoman here at midnight. Batman wanted her out of the way, just as she'd wanted him out of the way when she summoned him. But why? The icon. 208 Broad Street. Eddie Lobb.

"It won't work," Catwoman promised the air around her. "I'll find you. Come midnight, wherever you are, I'll be there first."

CHAPTER
Eighteen

C ATWOMAN needed her costume. Selina wanted her old familiar clothes, all of which were back at home. She stuffed the costume into a paper bag along with a few cans of tuna fish to fortify her during the wait, then she kicked her new clothes into the closet. She mussed her perfect hair with a moment of raking and shaking. The cats, who had stayed scarce since she stormed through the door, came forward to be petted. They climbed into her lap and let her know that they forgave her strange behavior of the last week or so.

"I won't forget who I am," she assured them, scratching each forehead a final time before pushing them all aside and getting to her feet. "Or why."

There were several hours of sunlight left in the afternoon when Selina began her reconnaissance of the empty warehouse at 208 Broad Street. The bloodstains were gone from the sidewalk, along with the ubiquitous yellow police tape. If she looked she could see where some of the painted bricks were freshly chipped—but only because she knew what to look for. Otherwise there was no sign that anyone had been near the place in months. She climbed up to the roof and studied the view. Along one direction of Broad Street she could see the three blocks down to the waterfront—the gaping fronts of Piers 21 and 22, a bit of Pier 23. All other directions were limited by the angles of the nearby streets to two blocks or less. When she was satisfied that she had the drop on both Batman and Eddie Lobb, she sat cross-legged on the capstones and popped open a can of tuna fish.

An hour went by, and traffic began to get heavier. She couldn't be certain she saw everything that came in sight of the building. She didn't see any capes; that was most important. When the rush hour slacked off she opened her second can of tuna. Most of the time she looked up Broad Street, away from the waterfront and the glare of the setting set. It was the direction from which Eddie had appeared before; it seemed likely that it was where he'd appear this time. It was pure chance that had her looking toward the waterfront as a pair of men walked away from Pier 23. She hadn't seen enough of Eddie to be certain of his silhouette or movement pattern, but a cat had to trust her curiosity. Stuffing her mouth with the last of the tuna fish and grabbing the bag containing the costume, Selina scrambled down to the street.

Since neither Eddie nor Batman would recognize her out of the Catwoman costume, Selina boldly set her pace to overtake the ambling men once she had them in sight again. She was still a half-block behind them when they turned away from the piers. They walked directly in front of her and she got a clean look at both their faces. They were both slightly sunburned and in need of shaves. One was an older man, heavyset and grizzled; the other one was unmistakably Eddie Lobb. Their eyes met by coincidence. Selina's heart skipped a beat, but there was nothing like recognition in Eddie's glance, only a predator's evaluation of potential prey. Selina noted that she failed to rate a second glance.

There'd be time for that later.

She strained her ears to hear their conversation as she passed behind them, but they were talking too softly, or not talking at all. Taking no chances, she kept going until she reached an alley, then went topside and tried to recapture their trail. They'd disappeared, and she had to do a street-level search until she found the dingy bar where, by all appearances, they were going to drink beer and watch the play-offs until midnight got closer.

"You have a good time," Selina urged as she cased the immediate area for another perch. "It'll be your last." With Batman putting himself back into the picture, along with the Feds tomorrow, she had to take whatever opportunity she got to finish him tonight.

Making herself comfortable on another roof, Selina waited until twilight became night before abandoning her street clothes and pulling the Catwoman costume around her. The dingy bar got the lion's share of the local activity. Men came and went at a steady rate, sometimes in groups but more often alone. Cabs disgorged passengers a handful of times during the long evening, but never anyone Catwoman remembered from the other evening. Eddie was still inside, and so was his partner. She guessed it was about ten when a squadron of police vehicles zoomed along the piers. They seemed to be going somewhere in a hurry, but they weren't spinning lights or sirens. She listened an extra moment or two without hearing anything conclusive, then forgot about them.

Another hour went by. The bar door opened and the grizzled man came out and promptly began a thorough scan of his surroundings. Catwoman flattened herself on the capstones. In this light, amid these old buildings, whatever lumps her silhouette added to the roofline shouldn't be recognizably human. Eddie emerged and exhibited none of his companion's caution before starting toward the piers. With a final glance over his shoulder, the companion fell in step.

Catwoman couldn't get a handle on the older man. He seemed to be smarter than Eddie; at the very least, he was suspicious while Eddie was not. He could cause complications, but, then again, he seemed to be taking orders. Well, it wouldn't be the first time a lesser man was in charge. Catwoman went over the wall at the back of the roof and traveled overland until she was above Broad Street across from number 208. She'd traveled fast and was unconcerned that there was no none in sight, but as minutes passed and no one showed up she realized that she was in the wrong place.

She backtracked to her lookout above the bar, then down the street to the piers. The concrete field where commuters parked their cars by day was nearly empty. There was no way across it except in plain sight. Catwoman strained her eyes, trying to convince herself that there was someplace else where Eddie and his friend were likely to be, but nothing else sprang to mind. She pumped her lungs with oxygen, then sprinted across the barren pavement to Pier 20.

The piers were new territory for Catwoman, and she quickly decided she didn't like them. The piers themselves were huge and hollow. Their floors were wooden; the boards shifted under her weight and she could hear water lapping beneath them. The water smelled of death; the remnants of her fish dinner turned acid in her gut. She could hear rats scurrying ahead of her. When something brushed lightly against her cheek she almost panicked: The rafters were filled with bats. Real bats.

She kept going, checking out the piers in order. Pier 21 was just as bad. Pier 22 was a bit worse, with something coarse and crunchy, like cat litter, grinding beneath her feet. With each step she hated Eddie a little bit more—he was the one making her endure this—and Batman. She emerged from Pier 22 at the foot of Broad Street. There were more cars parked here, unattended, quiet, and empty. Still, she entered Pier 23 more cautiously, and was glad she did.

The cavernous building echoed with distant voices. Light shone through a gap in the wall near the back. Unidentifiable silhouettes moved within it. Catwoman worked her way to the back of the pier, concealing herself in the shadows. Halfway back the silhouettes resolved into Eddie Lobb and his unknown companion. They had hoisted a car-sized sealed and wrapped crate into the pier. As the light came mostly from outside and below, Catwoman assumed the crate had come from a boat moored alongside the pier. Remembering their sunburnt, unkempt appearances, she assumed that the two men had been on the boat earlier. They were talking as they

worked, but with the echo it was impossible to decipher what
they were saying.

Catwoman eased closer. Something light and fleeting
struck her shoulder. She brushed herself off with short, vio-
lent strokes, cursing every bat, large or small, that had ever
flown. But it was a piece of paper, not something organic and
revolting. A gum wrapper, still reeking of spearmint. Her
heart was in her throat as she retreated and looked up. The
light was bad, and she didn't know what she should be seeing.
There were a number of black, bulky shapes above her, but
nothing she could interpret. She thought of Batman and made
herself alert for the subtle shimmer of his cape. Something
did move. It wasn't Batman's cape and at first Catwoman had
no idea what it could have been, then she realized she was
looking at a man from the soles of his feet on up. Once she
had a coherent pattern in her mind, spotting other men was
child's play. There were at least four men hiding in the jumble
of rafters and catwalks some thirty feet above the pier's
wooden floor. One of them might be Batman, but Catwoman
wouldn't have put money on it.

The two men working on the crate gave no indication that
they were aware of their audience—even the older guy,
who'd been so careful coming out of the bar, seemed oblivi-
ous. The whole setup stank worse than the harbor water. It
was even possible that Batman's clumsy message had been a
sincere attempt to warn her away from a bad situation. It was
possible that Batman wasn't here, and wouldn't be here. At
another time Catwoman might have reconsidered her own
presence, but not this time.

Catwoman was close enough now to hear Eddie clearly.
He described the places he'd been and the jobs he'd done.
If there were cops hidden in the rafters, they might find it
interesting, but Catwoman found it boring. So, it seemed, did
the older man. He made the right noises at the right time,
without actually participating in the conversation. Between
the two of them they'd gotten the wrapping off the crate.
They removed the contents—smaller crates—and spread

them across the floor. Catwoman took note of the military stencils covering most of the smaller crates.

Weapons, she thought, sinking down on her haunches. Bonnie had blathered that the Feds weren't really interested in Eddie because he collected poached tiger relics. Selling U.S. hardware to terrorists, without government approval, was different. Catwoman glanced into the rafters again. The space was lousy with human shapes. She caught a brief glint of metal; someone had unholstered his gun.

It must be getting close to midnight.

She chose her final position, against the outer wall on the far side of the crate, looking back the length of the pier. She was not alone; there was a man with a gun crouched between her and the crate. The damned wooden planks creaked beneath her feet. The crouched man turned around. He should have seen her; he must have seen her silhouette, but he did nothing about it. Catwoman was relieved, and she was disturbed: if her own presence raised no alarm, how many men were hiding in the shadows? Did they all know each other? What were they expecting? What were they planning to do?

There was no time for guesses. A rattletrap vehicle was making a noisy approach to the pier. Its headlights held everyone motionless as it jolted from the concrete and asphalt onto the wooden planks. The entire structure vibrated as it roared toward them. Catwoman dug her claws into the floor and prayed they weren't all going for a swim. The vehicle braked. The engine idled at an unhealthy whine as four men piled out with guns drawn and looking very nervous. The man in front of Catwoman drew his gun and held it steadily as he scuttled sideways into the deeper shadow directly behind the large crate. Catwoman followed, though it meant that she could no longer see what was happening.

"You will load in the back," a man said in thickly accented English. "Now, please. No arguments."

"You'll never make it to Canada in that clunker, Khalki." Catwoman recognized Eddie's voice. "Let's be reasonable— you take a look at what we've brought in. If you like it, we all get in the boat, we go out to where the rest of the merchandise is moored, we radio the captain of the *Atlantic Star*—''

"Please, no. My way now, not yours. You will load in the back."

"They're armed and they're antsy, Tiger. We better do what they say."

That voice must belong to the partner and Eddie must call himself Tiger. Catwoman wasn't surprised, merely more determined than ever that she was going to claim him tonight. She began circling wide behind the crate out of the headlight beams, toward the light-filled gap in the wall above the boat. In a moment, she could see the pale, anxious faces of the foreigners and Eddie walking boldly toward them, arms wide open and laughing. He was not without a certain crass courage.

"Khalki, friend, think about it. I'm offering you everything you want—everything you asked for, lifted out of the sea and loaded on a boat bound for Odessa."

If the foreigner had any brains at all, Catwoman judged, he wouldn't trust Eddie. And it looked like he did have brains, and a twitchy finger. Another step and Eddie was going to have a hole for a heart. This was not how she meant for Eddie to die. Catwoman balanced on her toes, not quite certain what she wanted to do, or if it could be done. As it turned out, the decision wasn't hers.

"Freeze!"

Switches were thrown and cones of light descended from a pair of hand-held spots in the rafters.

"This is the Gotham City Police Department. Drop your weapons. Raise your hands slowly."

The foreigners were stunned; so was Eddie. They looked into the light, blinding themselves. The older man wasn't surprised at all. He advanced toward Eddie. Then a gun was fired somewhere in the rafters. Khalki was thrown backward by the bullet impact. Then the spotlights, and the men holding them fell to the floor, and then all hell broke loose.

Catwoman scrambled for cover. Somebody shot out the headlights of the foreigner's truck. The only light in the pier came from the boat riding in the water some distance below. The gunman who'd been hiding in front of her aimed his weapon into the rafters. She didn't think he hit anything with his one round, but two other gunmen saw the muzzle flash. One shot got him in the neck. His death throes carried him into the light from below. When he collapsed on his back the letters "G C P D" were legible on his bulky vest. Eddie had drawn a weapon and was using the smaller weapon crates as a shield. He had the gun cocked but was too busy dodging to take aim or fire. The older man was nowhere in sight. The three remaining foreigners were using their ancient pickup truck for cover and firing wildly into the darkness overhead.

There was nothing Catwoman could do except keep herself out of trouble, but then Eddie took a bullet in the shoulder. His gun went flying and he lay sprawled on his back, an easy target for every gunman on the floor or in the rafters. Screaming with pain and panic, Eddie thrashed on the planks, desperate to find his gun, to get to his feet.

Catwoman got to her feet so he would see her and recognize her before he died. She was shielded partially be her black costume and partially by overlapping shadows. Still, it was a risky move, a stupid move, but she was acting with her heart, not thinking with her head.

"Look at me, Eddie!"

He did, and he stopped screaming. He stopped groping for his gun. There was a lull in the chaos. Selina realized how exposed she was, how endangered her need for vengeance had made her, when something large and heavy struck her from the side, knocking her off her feet.

The lull ended. Lead was flying again, and Catwoman struggled to free herself from Eddie's partner, the old man who was as strong as a bull elephant and uncannily adept at avoiding her claws. Every move she made toward escape, he had a countermove to keep her in hand and push her another step toward the gaping door above the boat. Catwoman reached deep within herself, summoning all her strength and will for one more assault. His face was a hand span from hers.

Batman.

Catwoman's discipline and training failed her. She lashed out with wild anger, and he dodged her easily.

"You don't belong here!" he said in a coarse whisper as he lifted her off her feet. "Hold your breath and don't swallow."

He threw her through the light-filled gap like a rag doll. There was nothing Selina could do except tuck herself into a ball and follow his instructions. She hit the water like a brick and sank for an eternity before she got her arms and legs moving upward. Gunplay continued far above her when she broke the water's surface, but for her the battle was over.

The river water was frigid. The tide was going out and the current was strong and already pulling her away from Pier 23. Water wasn't Catwoman's element. It was a struggle to keep calm and work her way toward the shore without smashing into one of the slime-and-barnacle-encrusted pilings. She was still navigating when she heard another body-sized splash behind her. Curiosity turned her around; the current pulled her under. She gave all her attention to survival after that.

CHAPTER
Nineteen

*H*OURS after hauling herself out of the freezing harbor, Selina crawled into her apartment. She was shivering from the cold and, she feared, from the onset of some river-borne disease. Despite Batman's warning, she'd swallowed more of the rank, salty water than she cared to remember. Several bouts of nausea had prolonged her journey home. All the horror stories she'd ever heard about people dying after one swallow of Gotham's polluted water elbowed to the front of her memory. Since arriving in the City she'd only been seriously sick—as opposed to seriously beaten—once, during her first winter here. That was when she'd discovered the mission.

The thought that she might wind up there again refueled the nausea. Selina staggered to the bathroom and wretched until her gut was sore. Then she turned on the shower and sat beneath it with the warm water pelting her face.

If the harbor water did make her sick, Selina decided that she'd call Bonnie. That woman would think of something, and the price of friendship was easier to bear than going back to the mission. The shivering finally stopped and she felt well enough to peel the costume off. She scrubbed it thoroughly, trying not to notice the brownish water swirl down the drain, and left it in its usual place to dry. Then, wrapped in towels and blankets, she lay across her bed in the dark, thinking about Eddie and thinking about Batman.

Whoever would have thought that Batman was an old man with graying hair and puckery, alcoholic's mottled skin and wrinkles in his cheeks? She remembered all the times she'd changed her plans because of him—a man on the downhill side of fifty! Then she remembered how he'd tossed her off the pier.

You don't belong here; those were his very words. It was almost as if he'd been protecting her like a father.

Selina shuddered and pulled the pillow over her head. She was fantasizing about having Batman for a father! She really must be getting sick. Batman hadn't protected her; he'd come between her and Eddie Lobb. He'd been protecting Eddie! A muscle spasm put knots in Selina's stomach. She ground her teeth together and waited for the pain to pass. In her mind's eye the world was a mass of writhing, eel-y things with gaping, round mouths and sharp teeth. The spasms struck again, worse than before. She knew her thoughts were making her sick. She tried to redirect them or, when that failed, to make her mind go blank. She got rid of the eel-y things, but not Eddie Lobb and not Batman. Their faces continued to haunt her as she fell into a restless sleep.

She awoke with a jolt many hours before she wanted to. Dream wisps tangled her thoughts, leaving her disoriented. Selina didn't recognize her surroundings. She didn't know where she was, or who she was, or what that infernal ringing was. Then her mind cleared enough to identify the telephone. She thrashed free of the bed coverings and answered it automatically.

"Selina! Have you seen the papers? You've got to read them. Turn on your television!"

The female voice was familiar. When Selina was able to match it to Bonnie's name and image, everything else snapped into place: her own name, her home, where she had been all night, and what Bonnie was chattering about.

"The Feds waited until the TV crews were ready. They're going in right now; it's live on the National News Network. Oh, Selina—don't tell me you don't have a television. Hurry up and come up to the Warriors office, you can watch from here. Oh! There's the table. They're bringing out the table! It's all because of what happened last night."

"What do you mean 'because of what happened last night'?" Selina kicked away the last clinging blanket. Her stomach remained sore from all the retching, but otherwise she felt fine. Angry and suspicious, but physically fine. She began to pace.

Bonnie made an exasperated noise. "Right. Yeah, I forgot—you don't know there was a big shoot-out on the waterfront last night, because Catwoman was there and you're not Catwoman."

Selina stopped pacing. "Who says Catwoman was anywhere last night?"

"It's in all the papers. It's even on 3-N. Eyewitnesses—policemen—who say they saw you—her—step out of the shadows and then get thrown into the water. It's not like there're pictures, but everybody saw you—her. Everybody who lived, anyway."

"What about Eddie Lobb?" Selina abandoned her pretenses. Bonnie already knew her secrets, and Bonnie knew what was going on. "I saw him get shot, but not what happened afterward. Was he one of the ones who lived or one of the ones who didn't?"

The rustling newspaper created static on the line. "It just says that Eddie—they call him 'Edward, a.k.a. Tiger, Lobb'—was identified by the suspects and police as the man who followed Catwoman into the water. 'Although the pier was immediately cordoned off and the search continued until after sunrise, Mr. Lobb could not be found. Divers will search the water around the pier later in the day. However, unnamed sources at the police department suggest that Catwoman may have played a role in Mr. Lobb's apparent escape.' "

Selina shook her head wearily. Whether it was the police or the media, they never got her role in anything right. "Unnamed because they're stupid and wrong," she snarled at Bonnie. "I could tell them a thing or two about who was helping Eddie Lobb get away!"

Bonnie was enthralled by the possibility.

Selina was appalled to hear the words her own voice was saying. "Later," she corrected. "I'll tell you later. We'll do dinner. But now you've got to let me do what I've got to do—" She waited for Bonnie to react.

"Okay—I'll make tapes of everything. You can tell me how stupid and wrong everyone is. It'll be our secret."

"Maybe," Selina said as she hung up the receiver. She lingered beside the phone, expecting it to ring again, expecting that she would have to ignore it, but it remained inert.

The costume was nearly dry. Selina pulled it on carefully and folded the mask hood under the neck band and wrestled with the wrist seams. The gloves could be folded up under the sleeves, although she could count the number of times she'd bothered to do so on the fingers of one hand. She rarely layered the costume beneath her mundane clothes; even in the dead of winter she preferred to shed one identity completely before adopting the other. But not today. Today Selina wanted Catwoman with her.

Batman was alone in Commissioner Gordon's City Hall office. The raid had been ruled a success, despite the gunplay. The two policemen who fell from the rafters were in the hospital; their lives had been saved by the elasticity. The officer who'd taken the fatal neck wound was being named a hero who'd fallen in the line of duty. Today that didn't lessen the anguish of his grieving family, but in time it might.

As for the others: Khalki, the Gagauzi leader, was in temporary serious condition. The remaining three Gagauzi had been arrested, but the story of their tiny community's struggle for identity and independence was capturing the hearts of those Americans who could always be counted on to root for the underdog. Even the Moldovans—the other men in the rafters whose unexpected presence had reduced Commissioner Gordon's carefully planned raid to chaos—garnered some sympathy for their desire to forge a reunited Rumania.

Commissioner Gordon had impounded the crates of weapons sitting in a Gotham pier. Batman, himself, had provided the navigational information necessary to retrieve the balance of the cache from its submerged mooring in international waters. A delegation from a handful of national agencies had already flown up from Washington, proverbial caps in their proverbial hands, to pay homage to Gotham's finest. He hadn't seen the Commissioner look so proud and happy in years.

There were only two people not satisfied with the way things had turned out. One was Bruce Wayne, who had hesitated a moment too long making certain that Catwoman had surfaced safely after he threw her into the harbor, and lost Eddie Lobb in the process. The other was, presumably, Harry Mattheson, who had, by now, certainly heard about the debacle on Pier 23 and surely could not be pleased with its outcome. It was possible that Harry believed the unsourced reports that Catwoman and Tiger were in cahoots.

Batman knew better.

A television sat in a corner of Commissioner Gordon's office. The volume had been muted, but the pictures scrolling across the screen—officials from the Justice Department and the Customs Office hauling that bone table and chair out of the Keystone—told Batman everything he needed to know about Catwoman's involvement with Tiger from the very beginning.

Batman used the phone behind Gordon's desk and dialed a direct line to the Batcave communications computer. Alfred was on the other end of the line almost immediately. It took a moment to assure the butler that he was in one, undamaged piece and to explain that he wasn't ready to come home.

"I've been watching television. I didn't know enough about Tiger. Batman's got to stop her."

There was a two-beat pause at the other end. "Are you certain, sir?"

"Yes, Alfred, I'm certain." He was always amazed at the

amount of concern the butler could pack into a few, supremely
polite words. He shouldn't have been. Alfred went along
with the Batman, but he had never completely accepted the
concept.

"Very well, sir. I'll be along presently."

Batman lowered the receiver. He cocked his head toward
the door and recognized the rhythm of Gordon's footsteps.

"Thanks for the use of the facilities, old friend," he said,
opening the door before Gordon could knock. "I feel like a
new man."

"You're always welcome here. You're sure I can't talk
you out of this? Lobb's body is probably going to show up
under the Harbor Mouth Bridge in a few days, and if it
doesn't, he's going to wish it had. The gumshoes over in the
Federal Prosecutor's office are ready to take Gotham apart
brick by brick to find their would-be canary. Word on the
street already is that Tiger's chopped liver."

"I've got to find him before someone else does."

Gordon wrinkled his nose as if the wind had just blown
something rotten past it. "You think she's innocent?"

He said nothing.

"Stay out of trouble," Gordon said as his guest departed.

Tiger came to thinking he was already in a prison; then he
realized that the room was too small to be a prison cell. He
was in Old Town. He'd come here looking for the almost-
doctor who'd fix anything for the right price. He must have
passed out when the sewing started. Tiger never had been a
tough man when it came to his own pain. He levered himself
into a sitting position. The hole in his shoulder felt like a bolt
of white-hot metal, but he could make everything move. A
stranger offered him an amber-colored bottle and a glass of
cloudy, suspect water.

"For the pain. Water now?"

Tiger pushed the glass away, but he took the pills in his
good hand. "Tell the quack I said thanks for the hospitality."

He couldn't stand up until he got into the passageway. The
sudden change in posture made him woozy, but there was no

going back. Not after last night. It had gone bad so quickly, so completely. He'd never believed the sheepherders when they said their enemies would stop at nothing. As far as he'd been concerned, they'd always belonged in a circus sideshow. And the police—who had tipped them? But then the black cat—the black tiger—had appeared, and he'd seen what he had to do. He got away alive. There was still hope.

The sun was high overhead when Tiger came out the unmarked metal door. It hurt his eyes. He'd been out longer than he thought. He reached reflexively for his sunglasses, but they were gone, along with his jacket and his shoes. The shoes he was wearing were too big. The jacket was too small and stank of chili sauce, but it covered the bloodstains on his shirt. He tugged on it a couple times, just to make sure, then headed for the street.

The Connection knew what had happened. There was no way the Connection didn't know by now. So Tiger was careful coming out of the alley. He checked both directions for the antenna-sprouting van. The street was clean. Tiger was just as cautious at the next intersection, and the one after that; then he began to relax. If the boss wanted to see him, the van would have been waiting for him. He wanted to get home and clean himself up before he met with the boss to square things up.

On the edge of Old Town he hailed a taxi and gave the Keystone address. The cabby dropped the flag and steered one-handed into traffic.

"You live in there?" the cabby asked, looking at Tiger in the rear seat, not at the traffic. "More kinds of cops parked over there than I ever seen before. Television cameras. The works. This guy they're after, he must really be something."

Tiger went numb. The pain in his shoulder was a world away. He told the cabby to let him out a few blocks shy of the Keystone. His hands were shaking as he dug into his emergency stash and produced a twenty.

"Keep the change."

"Thanks." The cabby rolled the bill with the hand that never touched the steering wheel and tucked it into his shirt pocket. "You know, you don't look so good. You sure you don't want me to get closer?"

"The fresh air'll do me good," Tiger replied with a thin-lipped smile. Feeling returned to his shoulder as he got out of the cab. He relieved his pain by slamming the door. The cabby told him to go to hell.

Tiger hoped that wasn't going to happen, but hope was fading.

Television vans were double-and triple-parked. None of them was big enough to be the boss's, but Tiger approached them cautiously just the same. There was no reason to panic, Tiger told himself as he neared the end of the line of vans and the start of the police cars. He'd had a bad day—a disastrous, catastrophic day—but nothing he did would justify this media circus.

"Can you move to one side, buddy? We're trying to film here."

A harried technician raised his hand at Tiger's wounded shoulder. Tiger backpedaled, but stayed in the crowd as the movie-star-handsome reporter called for a sound and light check. He couldn't keep from holding his breath as the tape began to roll.

"Who is Eddie—Tiger—Lobb? In one night he's gone from being a precinct nuisance to worldwide notoriety. Two things are clear. First, as the nation and the world saw earlier today, Eddie Lobb turned his Gotham City home into a conservationist's worst nightmare. And second, he was a major factor in the Pier 23 shoot-out that left one policeman dead, two injured, and made Bessarabia a household word. But who is Eddie—Tiger—Lobb? With me now is Ramon Diaz, the doorman here at the Keystone Condominiums—"

The reporter paused dramatically. Tiger was seized with fear. Rayme would recognize him standing here at the front of the crowd and it would be as good as over. The pause lengthened uncomfortably.

"Where the hell is he? Where's the little guy? Stop rolling."

Tiger recognized an eleventh-hour reprieve when he got

one. He melted back through the crowd. An all-too-human part of him refused to believe this was happening. Then a gap opened in the crowd farther up the block and he looked into the back of a moving truck. All his tigers were in there, jumbled together without any respect or order. They'd never forgive him for this. They'd destroy him. He was as good as dead. He'd have been better off staying in the river and letting the tide take him out to sea.

All the same, turning himself in to the dozens of waiting policemen never occurred to Eddie Lobb. If he had to die, he was going to die the way he'd lived, on the waterfront streets, not rotting in some jail. Miraculously, his mind had cleared and his shoulder was pain-free. Tiger had no difficulty slipping back down the block and hailing another cab.

"Take me over to the docks," he told the driver.

He got out at Pier 23—the old Blue Star Line. It was quiet, nothing to show for all the excitement. The Connection would survive. Tiger admitted—for the first and only time—that he wasn't a big enough man in the organization to take his boss down with him. But Pier 23 was as dead as he was. The boss would shut down all the operations that touched it. He stared at it awhile—a man needed to set things in his memory, even when he knew he wasn't going to remembering anything pretty soon. Then he ambled over to his favorite bar and sat at his favorite table.

"Hey, Tiger—you don't look so good."

One of the Pier 23 stevedores made himself comfortable in the chair opposite Eddie.

"Things went bad. You heard."

"Yeah, I heard. Tough break, Tiger. People been comin' in askin' about you."

"Cops?"

"Yeah, cops . . . and people. They gave me a message to give you, if you should show up."

"So, give."

"They says if you want to make things square again, you go over to the place on Broad Street. There, I give you the message. I give you a piece of advice, too—don't go over

there, Tiger. Get outta Gotham City. There must be a hundred
places you could go.''

"I ain't paying for advice, Jack.''

The stevedore got up from the table. "Then it's been swell
knowing you." He walked away.

Tiger finished his beer and left another twenty on the table
to pay for it. The place on Broad Street; he knew where that
was. The clarity that had come upon him by the Keystone
had been dulled a bit by the beer. His shoulder was throbbing
again and he was tired, too tired to go around the corner to
the place on Broad Street. Tiger decided to return to the
waterfront one last time. When the tide changed he'd make
the final journey. It seemed that all the nearby buildings had
eyes when he left the bar. Maybe the boss was going to have
him popped on the street. He forced the muscles in his back
to relax. The word was that it didn't hurt at all if you were
relaxed.

Batman paid little attention to the dead man as he walked
past. He was watching the roofs and the shadows for some
telltale glimmer of movement that would reveal Catwoman's
hiding place. A woman wearing sunglasses and a bright floral
print dress stepped out of a doorway. She didn't seem the
right type, but she was carrying a large purse and she was
following Tiger. Batman was armored within his costume. He
allowed himself the hope that Catwoman would be similarly
concealed when he found her. It would be easier for them
both if they handled this professionally. The woman changed
her bearings and headed for the parked cars. Batman combed
the shadows again.

The days were lengthening and getting warm. Batman was
forcibly reminded that the black polymer was a heat sponge
and unpleasant to wear in the sunlight. He'd guessed Tiger's
intention of sitting on a piling until the tide changed again,
which wouldn't happen until after sunset. Catwoman wasn't
likely to make her approach in broad daylight. The Wayne
Foundation owned a building not far from here where Batman
maintained a safe house. Instinct and logic agreed that he
could afford to snatch a couple hours of naptime. He didn't

owe Tiger anything, although the scar-faced man wouldn't be looking at a death sentence if their paths hadn't crossed. He didn't owe anything to Catwoman, either. But he stayed where he was, dulling his senses to the heat, waiting for the sun to set, the tide to change, and the final act in Tiger's drama to begin.

The temperature in the cul-de-sac where Batman had hidden himself dropped noticeably when the sun dropped below the roofline of the piers. Batman shook himself out of auto-pilot and assured his conscious mind that nothing had changed—Tiger still sat on his piling and Batman's criminal sense still told him Catwoman was near. Shadows lengthened and a scattering of streetlights sizzled to life. Isolated pools of halogen light emerged from the twilight. There was a movement, a shadow within a shadow, at the front of the pier nearest to Tiger. Batman became fully alert.

Tiger began moving. So did the shadow. So did Batman. They moved together toward Broad Street. Tiger started down the middle of the street. A piece of shadow separated from the piers. Batman adjusted his course for an intercept once she reached Broad Street. She slashed at his face when he forced her against a wall. The mask took the brunt of it, but one claw had found its mark and he felt a warm trickle across his cheek.

"It's over," Batman told her. He locked his hands firmly over her wrists and held the vicious hooks at arm's length.

Catwoman's face contorted with hate and fury. The twin passions stripped away her ability to speak. She hissed and growled like the alley animal she pretended to be. They were close enough to taste each other's breath.

"Do you want to *die* with him? He'd like that. He still thinks you're on his side—a figment of his 'tiger spirit.' "

Batman's arms were longer; when he straightened them, she couldn't move. The raw rage in Catwoman's face was tempered with fear. She couldn't take him in a fair fight. So she lashed out with her boots against his shins and drove her knee into his crotch. He bore the assault stoically, but he released her wrists. She made a bolt for the building Eddie had entered just as the ground lurched beneath her feet. She stood flat-footed, not believing her eyes, as the walls of 208 Broad Street bulged outward.

"Omygod," she whispered, sounding exactly like Bonnie.

Catwoman was hit from behind, not from the front, and spun around before the building blew itself to pieces. She was in the air, then she was in the dark, crushed flat against the asphalt pavement and barely able to breathe. For a moment Selina had no sense of her body. She feared the worst, then nerves from her fingers to her feet tingled and she knew she was all right. She thrashed free of the debris pinning her to the ground—bricks, mortar, wood, Batman. There was a wall of fire where 208 Broad Street had been. A gassy smell lingered in the air. The danger of another explosion was very real.

Her stunned consciousness finally deciphered what was lying at her feet. She planted her claws in the polymer armor and flipped Batman onto his back. His eyes were open and empty. His chest was heaving, but he wasn't making any noise. Neither was the fire. Selina realized the blast had deafened her. She screamed and felt the sound in her throat, but not in her ears. She turned and ran.

CHAPTER
Twenty

*B*ONNIE got Selina to a doctor, who assured her, in writing, that her hearing loss was temporary. Bonnie also invaded the East End with an armload of uptown take-out food and a bottle of the robust red wine that came in straw-wrapped bottles.

"You look like a ragpicker," Selina said when she opened the door. She spoke slowly and carefully. Her hearing was already partly restored, but she had a tendency to talk too loudly and her own voice sometimes echoed confusingly in her ears.

Bonnie said something Selina didn't catch on her way to the kitchen counter.

"What?"

"I look the way you always look," she repeated.

"That's no excuse."

Selina was uncomfortable at first. She expected Bonnie to do or say something that would reveal her contempt for the East End way of life. But Selina had never gone to college and lived off campus. Selina rarely drank, either. All her life she'd been surrounded by the ravages of alcoholism. There had been times when her only source of pride was the knowledge that she wasn't a drunk. Bonnie wasn't afraid of a glass of wine, and with Bonnie sprawled on the floor, playing with the gray tiger kitten and talking her usual blue streak, Selina dared tiny sips from a jelly glass.

The evening was the most pure, simple fun Selina had had with another person since—well, at least since she arrived in Gotham City. She told Bonnie the kitten was hers, if she wanted to take him home and give him a name. She did. The visit ended early, while Bonnie, carrying the kitten in a cardboard box, still had a prayer of hailing a taxicab on the avenues. Selina waved good-bye and returned home, still feeling warm and mellow.

"Maybe I shouldn't go out," she said to the cats. "Maybe I should just stay home and get some sleep."

The cats ignored her, and she dug Catwoman's costume out from under the bed. She had no fixed destination in mind, but wasn't surprised when she found herself looking at the Keystone's wedding-cake facade. The excitement was long over and just about forgotten. Somebody had given the police an anonymous tip about the Broad Street explosion, and the Federal Prosecutors had to start looking for another sleazeball to squeeze.

Catwoman wasn't sure what she expected to find—bare walls, new tenants—when she raised the window and slipped in behind the drapes. The mirror-ceiling bedroom had been searched, but not trashed. The wardrobe doors were shut and locked. It was clear to Catwoman, after that, why she'd come. She got out her picks. The doors swung open. The box was there. She lifted it out. It was filled with strands of pearls and semiprecious stones—none worth the trouble of fencing, so she left them in the box's place and closed the doors.

Somebody should tell the nuns to tell Rose that it was safe to go home again.

Selina had what she'd come for. The only other thing she was interested in—the velvet painting of the prowling tiger in the living room—was far too big to think about. She should have called it a night and headed home, but curiosity, as always, got the better of her and she opened the corridor door.

The door to Tiger's relic room lay on its side, blocking the closets. More to the point, a night-light's worth of foot-candles was spilling out of the room itself. Holding the box tightly against her side, Catwoman took a peek.

"I knew you would come. Sooner or later."

Selina was startled. She thought—hoped—her ears were playing tricks on her, but there he was in full regalia silhouetted against an undraped window. She put her right foot behind her left, and measured the distance to the gouged door frame with her outstretched hand.

"Don't go. I wanted to tell you that I didn't understand until it was too late. I knew you were involved, but I thought it was the icon, strictly business. I didn't know about this."

Eddie Lobb's sanctuary had been stripped to the bare walls, which concentrated the sound of Batman's voice, making it easy for her to hear him.

"What difference would it have made? Would you have let me have him? Ever?" The questions were as sharp as the claws she thrust into the wood behind her.

Batman gave them the decency of a moment's thought and an honest answer. "No. I wanted Tiger's boss. I still do. You were trying to destroy him. I had to stop you, if I could."

"You couldn't. He's dead and the trail's gone cold. I won."

Another pause. "In a way you did, I suppose. But you were lucky. Someday your luck will go sour."

"I'll take my chances."

"You're alone, Catwoman. You've got no one. It doesn't have to be that way."

Damn her quirky hearing! Catwoman swallowed hard and felt her ears pop. It didn't help. She couldn't hear all the nuances in Batman's voice. She couldn't be certain what he meant.

"I'm doing fine," she said defensively.

"You're not like the others. You don't have to wind up at the end of a blind alley."

Catwoman shifted her weight onto her right foot. This conversation was the only thing going up a blind alley. "Don't waste your time worrying about me," she snarled.

And was gone.

Batman let his breath out slowly. Alfred had warned him that Catwoman wasn't going to be persuaded by a halfhearted offer of friendship. It was all or nothing with cats. With Bruce Wayne, "all" went to Batman and there was nothing left over. He gave her enough time to get clear of the building before leaving the room himself.

Then the phone rang. The line was supposed to be dead. Bruce Wayne was curious. He picked it up.

"Is that you, Batman?" The voice was bland. "Come to gloat over your successes? You've made a nuisance of yourself, but you're not even close. Eddie Lobb, Tiger, had reached the end of his usefulness. You did me a favor. We're even again. There's no need for us to interfere with each other."

"We're not even. We never were. I know who you are, and I'm going to bring you down."

"Don't be a fool, Batman. You're not in my league."

"I'm not a fool, Mattheson. I'm Batman."

Breathtaking Batman® adventure from Warner Books!

Don't miss any of these extraordinary novels starring the Caped Crusader™—as he wages a never-ending battle against evil and injustice.

☐ **BATMAN: CAPTURED BY THE ENGINES**
by Joe R. Landsdale
(A36-042, $4.99 USA) ($5.99 Can.)

☐ **BATMAN**
by Craig Shaw Gardner
(A35-487, $4.95 USA) ($5.95 Can.)

☐ **THE BATMAN MURDERS**
by Craig Shaw Gardner
(A36-040, $4.95 USA) ($5.95 Can.)

☐ **BATMAN: TO STALK A SPECTER**
by Simon Hawke
(A36-041, $4.95 USA) ($5.95 Can.)

**Warner Books P.O. Box 690
New York, NY 10019**

Please send me the books I have checked. I enclose a check or money order (not cash), plus 95¢ per order and 95¢ per copy to cover postage and handling,* or bill my ☐ American Express ☐ VISA ☐ MasterCard. (Allow 4-6 weeks for delivery.)

___Please send me your free mail order catalog. (If ordering only the catalog, include a large self-addressed, stamped envelope.)

Card # _____

Signature _____ Exp. Date _____

Name _____

Address _____

City _____ State _____ Zip _____
*New York and California residents add applicable sales tax.   532